THE PATH TO PURGATORY

Book 2 of the Sibyl Chronicles

Marlene Pardo Pellicer

THE PATH TO PURGATORY: BOOK 2 OF THE SIBYL CHRONICLES. Copyright © Marlene Pardo Pellicer. First Printing 2020. Printed in the United States of America

First Edition:
First Printing

PUBLISHED BY ELEVENTH HOUR LLC
www.11thhour.company

E-BOOK ISBN 978-1-7348360-0-4
PRINT ISBN 978-1-7348360-1-1

DEDICATION

To my mother Ofelia Martinez, who passed away on December 28, 2019 at the age of ninety-one. I know that among all those that love me, none loved me as selflessly as she did. I was blessed to have her as my parent.

About The Author

Marlene is a native Miamian and has been writing since 1971, (on a manual typewriter when she was eleven years old).

She is the founder of *Miami Ghost Chronicles*, and a paranormal researcher since the 1990s. She is also the producer, host and narrator of *Stories of the Supernatural*, *Nightshade Diary* and *Supernatural StoryTime* podcast series, and the blog author of *Stranger Than Fiction Stories*.

Marlene lives with her husband Henry (AKA official sandwich maker for starving authors) on a micro-farm and bee sanctuary in Miami's 100-year-old agricultural belt, surrounded by several dogs (AKA writing companions), various noisy exotic birds, a large flock of equally noisy free-range chickens and a very quiet rescue rabbit named Thelma.

If you'd like to receive my newsletter announcing specials, updates on new books and requests for ideas, please sign up on my website.

www.MarlenePardo.com

Other Books by Marlene

FICTION
Diabolique: A Sibyl Novella (2019)
Walker Between the Worlds: Book 1 of the Sibyl Novella (2019)

NON-FICTION
Haunted History of the Old West's Wicked Ladies & The Bad Hombres They Loved (2017)
The Lady in the Blue Kimono: Film Noir Murders (2018)
Supernatural Safety: A Paranormal DIY Guide (2018)

There is a charm about the forbidden that makes it unspeakably desirable.

Mark Twain

References

Sempiterno Apostasy - *A secret sect that infiltrated the Vatican because stories of unearthly and evil creatures were acknowledged and catalogued there. Their members include a select few known as the Dispossessed. Touched by Evil at some time in their lives, their minds were open to the world beyond. They could see its inhabitants, and in turn be seen by them. Who comprised this sect became one of the most sought after secrets in the Vatican. Even the most powerful cardinals and the Inquisition feared them. Members lived in all parts of the world, and their exact number remains unknown even to the Dispossessed themselves.*

Pocket—*a human avatar used by a spiritually advanced being or a demon to disguise their likeness.*

Contents

PROLOGUE

The hurricane raged and grew as it gyrated over the warm waters of the Caribbean Sea. Antillean islands in its path suffered for it. The uninhabited ones were fleeced of trees. Coconut palms cracked and were hurled into the surf. Humans, who lived on the inhabited islands, looked with longing eyes at birds that took flight and escaped death. Crops were ruined, and houses demolished, but what did that matter if you were dead?

Fed by the loss of life, human, animal and plant, it roared unto the Yucatán Peninsula at approximately 200 miles per hour. Still hungry it devoured the land and everything on it. Its path through the vine-trailed jungles of British Honduras left mahogany trees toppled, and places once obscured by rainforest growth saw the light of day in hundreds of years.

Finally satiated it allowed the mountainous terrain of Mexico to conquer it.

Charles Kydd's machete hacked its way through the jungle that only weeks after the storm, started once more to reclaim its territory. A howler monkey's call, unusual for this time of day, caused him to look around and gauge what time it was. He looked up at the sun and guessed the workers had another hour before nightfall. Then they would prudently retreat to the logging camp where safety lay in numbers, and the bright fire kept danger at bay.

He swung down again, and the jarring meeting of the blade against stone threw it from his grasp. Once retrieved, he hung it on his belt, and with questing fingers he pulled thin vines away.

The man gasped in surprise when a large, square stone fashioned by human hands erupted from the undergrowth. Further exploration displayed what appeared to be a wall.

He heard a step behind him, and saw that it was Tobias, a Kekchi Maya that worked as part of his crew felling mahogany trees.

"Tobias, come and look at what I have found."

The slender man with thick dark hair stepped next to him and looked down in silence. "Mr. Kydd, leave with me now. We should not be here."

"This is an exciting discovery. It's a ruin of some type."

Tobias' eyes widened with fear as he searched the surrounding jungle. Then they heard the deep rumble of a jaguar's roar.

"This is a cursed place, come away," Tobias urged.

Charles Kydd stopped his reply, when the animal's snarl instead of coming from the jungle, sounded as if it came from deep within the group of etched stones.

1. Death Rides a Horse Named Zabuca

CALIFORNIA, 1870.

Rain spattered hard on the muddy road and an unexpected layer of freezing fog cloaked itself over the sea. Night arrived prematurely.

The two figures on horseback held their cloaks close against their bodies and rode steadily toward the flickering light coming from an isolated tavern. Spindly trees cleared away from the entrance, and the smell of dried pine needles mingled with the smoky odor of a wood-burning fire.

One man said, "Father, let us stop here for the night."

The other one who wore a hat with a wide brim, just nodded his head.

They both dismounted, and the taller one took both horses by the bridle and led them towards the stable. The other entered a main room where a potbelly stove squatted unlit in the corner. A solitary candle winked from the mahogany bar, and embers glowed in the hearth. The tavern keeper slumped against a wall, dozing in its warmth. He roused himself and came over to help the visitor remove his cloak. He took his hat as well and hung them up so they could dry. The traveler was older, his creased face littered with a day's growth of gray stubble.

The saloon would normally be full of travelers and miners, but now it was empty. The morning was lovely, with the air clear and warm. The sky was blue with fleecy clouds, but as the day wore on the breeze, brisk before noon strengthened and filled the air with dust. Toward sundown the sky became overcast, with a gloomy cloud hanging about as low as the housetops. The wind howled like a hurricane, darkening the air with dirt and litter and the temperature fell thirty degrees in an hour.

A failed miner, once a soldier who spent his day at the tavern sipping coffee, telling stories and ribald jokes, fled to a more populated area with many of the patrons and all the employees. Before leaving he put his hand on the tavern keeper's shoulder and whispered, "Arthur, this unusual weather is a harbinger of dangerous times. If you insist on staying, do not open your door tonight. Be safe my friend."

So it was that the innkeeper found himself with two weary travelers as his only guests.

* * *

Mort Peccatum undid the flank cinch on Zabuca's saddle. With practiced hands he rubbed down both horses and led them to dry stalls. He thought it unusual there was not even a stable hand to help.

He hoped he made the right decision to stay at the inn. For several days he'd seen dust hanging on the trail behind them like somebody wanted to keep close without catching up. Mort knew this only meant trouble.

On the second day he made sure they left before daybreak, leaving the fire burning low so they would see the smoke in the morning light. They headed towards a little known pass. He cut back and forth through the brush until he found another trail headed northward. They stopped that night on an outcropping that gave him a vantage point towards the south and east.

2

THE PATH TO PURGATORY

The following day he lagged well past the time he usually rode on. There was no mistaking the dust cloud that puffed up southeast from their position. A closer inspection through field glasses showed four figures on horseback. They rode past the turnoff he took, realizing too late what he did. By their actions Mort could tell they were scouting to find the trail where they lost him, which started at the bottom of a wash.

Then earlier today, they rode towards buzzards that flew in a lazy circle above their find. Before long they come upon what attracted them. The stagecoach destined to stop at the tavern lay on its side down a canyon. The horses were driven off, and the driver lay face down in the dust; shot twice in the back. A couple dead... passengers. After inspecting the bodies, Mort scanned the surrounding rocks, but he felt no eyes sighting down a Winchester to pick him off. He crouched and looked at the tracks around the remains. They demonstrated that four men had been there, one wearing moccasins not used by any of the local tribes.

Mort realized that trouble trailed behind them and ahead of them as well, and they left the dead unburied with only a hasty blessing from the priest. He knew there were renegades that drifted down from Oregon or Nevada, raiding ranches or mining settlements for supplies, but they would not chase two riders who appeared to have nothing of value. He suspected his pursuers were not these types of men.

That day they rode hard not stopping once, and he felt sorry for the old padre, but he hoped to reach this old saloon and hotel. He also had not counted on the strange weather, and he was glad they could sleep with a roof over their heads.

Mort closed a stall door and stopped when he heard what sounded like the jingle of a harness from outside the barn. He stepped into a pocket of shadow outside the glow of the hanging lantern. Dressed all in black he melted into the inkiness. He peered between the slats of a smaller door of the wooden structure.

Four riders cantered their horses into the clearing. They look bedraggled and sodden, their horses not much better. Mort could see they'd been sleeping round a campfire instead of a room somewhere. He was sure these were their pursuers.

One of them, heavyset and taller than the rest had something familiar about him; he carried a gun low on his waist as if he used it frequently to end disputes. Mort tried to place him, but they went inside and he lost sight of the men. They left their horses tethered outside under the icy drizzle. Then a light streamed from an upstairs window. He guessed the innkeeper had taken Padre Salazar up to a room.

Mort pondered a moment. Should he stay and deal with them, or leave? They wanted only one thing. It was the item the priest had carried in a stained leather satchel through British Honduras and Mexico. He knew they did not plan to leave any witnesses alive.

Keeping to the shadows he crept up to the front window of the saloon and peered inside. The four men were at the bar drinking liquor and talking amongst themselves. The priest was gone. He guessed that right about now they were wondering if he and the priest had stopped or kept riding into the night, but they could not pass up the chance to warm themselves even for a while.

Mort walked to the back of the tavern, looking for the kitchen door. He hoped there would be a servant's staircase leading to the upper floor. The door swung open into darkness, and next to the cooking hearth, a slim layer of embers lighted the first narrow steps which disappeared into the gloom above. He crept up and knocked at a door with a stream of light winking out from underneath it. He heard the rustle of cloth and the click of a hammer being drawn back.

"Padre, it's me."

The door opened a crack and the barrel of a colt revolver emerged. The man lowered it when he saw who it was.

Mort whispered in a few words they were leaving. The priest pulled his cloak and hat from a nearby hook and followed the tall man quietly down the stairs and out into the moist night air. The rain ceased, but lightning flashed inside an approaching cloud bank accompanied by the roar of thunder.

Inside the stable, Mort saddled their mounts and led them outside. Once they were under the cover of the trees, he returned and untied the four horses of the men inside. He looked through the moisture-streaked glass and saw them sitting at a table. No doubt the keeper told them he and the priest took a room upstairs. They appeared in no hurry to confront him, believing their quarry was upstairs readying to sleep.

The boom of a thunderclap covered the noise of his movements and the squeaking of leather as he led their horses into the stable. Once the men discovered they were riderless, it would take them a long while to find the animals inside the barn. If he loosed them, they would only wander back looking for food and water.

Mort and his companion came to a swift creek that flowed deeper than it usually did because of the rainfall. They walked the horses across, and Mort held his gun belt and rifle high. On the other side, the horses scrambled up the bank.

He mentally debated over his earlier predicament; should he continue to ride through the night with inclement weather obscuring the trail, or face their pursuers. Mort reminded himself that the priest's safety was paramount and he could not risk him being shot in a gunfight.

The thunderheads flashed again, pushed along by increasing winds. Then he saw him, leaning against the trunk of a lightning struck tree. The man's face was chalky white, drained of blood. The

5

eyes, dark and shiny, were open wide and unblinking, red-rimmed and without expression. His clothing was a hodgepodge of dirty coat, pants and scuffed boots. The stained hat rolled at the rim, sat back on his head. Silently he beckoned Mort to follow him with an outstretched arm.

The priest looked with questioning eyes at the man standing next to him staring into the darkness. He squinted trying to make out what was there, but all he saw was the limbs of a barren tree.

Mort followed the miner, leading Zabuca by the reins, and Padre Salazar with the other horse trailed behind. The hollow sound of hooves against rock emphasized the skittering of falling pebbles behind them. The path thinned out and climbed until it suddenly leveled out. Perched on a small clearing was a dilapidated shanty. A lean-to sagged against an outer wall which once offered protection to the man's donkey or mules. The sound of the creek tumbling downwards swished close by.

Padre Salazar brushed by him and threw open the door. He declared over his shoulder, "No one has lived here for some time. It's dry though."

Mort once more stripped the saddles from the horses. The wind picked up, spattering thick drops against him. The miner appeared on the edge of the encampment. He glowed in the murkiness and with the same somber expression untied a scarf around his neck. A deep gash dripped blood.

Mort said in a hushed voice, "Peace be with you, I will be your witness."

The dead man nodded once and stepped back into the shadows and melted into nothingness.

Inside the cabin Padre Salazar started a fire that crackled in the small fireplace. Mort brought in their saddlebags and bedding. It surprised him to find pieces of cold chicken and bread sitting on a rough hewn wooden plate.

In answer to his unspoken question, Father Salazar explained, "I brought this food with me to the room, and I thought it wise not to leave it behind. We must eat."

Mort grunted and sat down on one of two worn chairs. A table and a narrow cot were the only other furnishings.

The older man motioned to the corner, "There's enough wood there to keep the fire lit for the night. Whoever lived here left unexpectedly."

"I imagine he did."

"Come, let us eat."

The man bowed his head and prayed his thanks for the food. Then he turned to Mort, "How did you find this place? There was no hesitation in your steps; it was as if you followed someone."

"I did, and when I discover his name, I will ask you to pray for his soul."

The old man stopped the question that sped to his tongue. They warned him that his protector was chosen precisely because he dealt in the turbulent and unseen world between the living and the dead.

Once they ate, he allowed the priest to take the cot, and he rolled out bedding on the floor. He placed his Henry rifle within arm's reach. His saddlebags became a pillow, and there was one that felt warm to the touch, as if it was a living thing. He traced the sigils that Ema burned into the leather, invoking their power to keep whoever carried it safe from evil.

He turned to Father Salazar, "I'll keep the fire burning for a few hours, but before dawn breaks we must put it out. We cannot afford to have smoke seen."

The priest nodded and laid back. Within a few minutes, his snores filled the small confines of the room.

Mort stretched out his long frame on the blankets. He looked at the door of the cabin and the thick piece of lumber that barred it from the inside. Whoever lived here wanted to make sure he was safe during those hours he slept. His last thoughts before drifting off to sleep were that despite the miner's efforts someone murdered him.

The wind pummeled the structure, and thunder exploded overhead. Mort cracked his eyes. The fire burned down low and he threw another log into it. Father Salazar slept deeply, and as he stretched back out, he realized where he saw the heavyset man that arrived at the tavern earlier in the night.

2.   Rancho Las Margaritas

Less than a week ago he rode into Rancho Las Margaritas, held by the powerful Robles family. It was only one of three ranches the family owned that covered in total over 200,000 acres. He knew that Don Santiago Robles, the family patriarch died a month before. He was a very hard man, except to his family. His widow agreed to receive Father Salazar until his escort arrived to guard him on his trek northward through California.

As was the custom, they welcomed Mort, but he sensed from the first meeting with the family that the apparent calm masked a great turmoil.

Don Robles' widow was young. Slim, of medium height she had a way about her that inspired desire in a man. She had creamy skin and a full mouth, and Mort found his eyes sliding back to her every time he looked away. She was obviously a lady, dressed in her widow's weeds; however everything about her warned him he should leave Rancho Las Margaritas as soon as possible. She was trouble, whether or not she meant to be. However he could not ride away within hours of arriving.

Don Robles' eldest son Marco stood next to his step-mother, and it was obvious he was senior to her by several years. He wore a short jacket made of calico silk, and a white linen shirt underneath with a black handkerchief knotted loosely around his neck. A red sash around his waist decorated black pants made of broadcloth.

Shoulder length hair graying at the temples coupled with dark piercing eyes gave him an aristocratic look.

Marco's wife sat next to him, and her eyes darted jealously to her husband every time he leaned over to speak to Maria Elena Robles. It appeared the dead man took a young bride in his later years.

Marco Robles eyed the tall, fair-haired stranger. His light blue eyes were direct, but did not disclose any emotion. He dressed like a gentleman; from the quality of the horse he rode to the fine stitching on his saddle and the holster encasing his rifle. His outfit was minimal and severe but cut from rich cloth and in excellent taste. Was he perhaps interested in purchasing land?

"Welcome Mr. Peccatum, we are glad to offer you our hospitality as we do to all travelers. Is there anything else you might need on your journey, directions, additional food…?"

Mort took off his black, low-crowned hat, and bowed his head to the ladies. His voice was deep and even, "Thank you for your offer Don Robles, however I believe you have misunderstood the reason for my presence. I am here to escort Padre Salazar into California."

Maria Elena Robles' black eyes grew enormous and her lips turned pale, like if she'd seen a ghost. Her voice was sharp when she said, "We expected a holy man to be his companion."

Mort harbored a sneaking feeling that she knew something about what Father Salazar carried with him.

Then a bearded monk walked in and upon seeing Mort threw back his cowl and greeted him with a powerful hug and a thump on his back. He commented in obvious satisfaction, "Mort, it is good to see you."

"You look well, old man, I mean Hermano Miel." Mort said with a laugh, warmth flooded the expression in his eyes.

"Hombre, I might be old, but I have old man strength, and the wisdom of years, quite a formidable combination to battle Satan with."

THE PATH TO PURGATORY

Brother Miel was a mystery even for those who knew him. He belonged to the mendicant order of Brothers of Charity de San Hipólito. His actual name was Richard, and famed for his knowledge as a beekeeper he became known as Richard Honey. Born in Ireland, he ended up in Spain and assumed the name of Ricardo Miel. Mort wasn't sure when he became a member of the Sempiterno Apostasy, but rumors were that prior to taking holy orders he had hired out as a mercenary to different armies across Europe.

Now as a mendicant he traveled across Mexico in a lifestyle of poverty. The order avoided owning property, embraced the poor and depended on the goodwill of those they preached to for survival. He was a perfect spy for the Church, but his loyalty lay with the Sempiterno Apostasy.

Both men turned to Padre Salazar. Brother Miel introduced Mort to him. "He will accompany you to your destination, and I can think of no one better for this task."

Padre Salazar nodded with tired eyes at the tall, blonde man. He carried a large leather satchel, worn and stained, with wide straps that criss-crossed his chest. Mort could see the weight of it had dug a groove into his shoulder.

Mort's eyes unbidden slid down to the pouch which for a moment seemed to pulse with movement, as a child makes inside its mother's belly. Then drops of blood, ruby red and viscous gathered at a corner and dripped to the floor.

The tall man did not react; knowing only he could see this imagery.

Brother Miel whispered low, "We must speak, alone."

Mort nodded, and they both turned back to their hosts.

"Forgive my rudeness, Doña Robles but I had not seen Mr. Peccatum in many years, and my heart is glad to set eyes upon him again."

11

Maria Elena Robles looked at both men with a speculative gleam in her eyes. "Very well, then I hope you will both entertain us with stories when we gather for dinner. Our servant will take you to your rooms so you may rest and then come for you later."

A servant girl with long glossy braids guided them out of the parlor. They followed her down a hallway with weathered tiles that gleamed reddish in the afternoon sun. They left Father Salazar in one room, and then both men excused themselves and stepped out into an enclosure with several steps that lead into a yard with a corral in the distance and other outbuildings.

The old friar took two letters from a satchel and handed them to Mort. He lowered his voice and his eyes darted around to make sure no one could overhear their conversation.

"One is for you and the other is for La Dama Roja. They are from Charles Kydd in British Honduras and came to me from someone different other then Father Salazar. The only instruction is that you should read them once you reached your destination in San Francisco."

Mort slid them into the inner pocket of his jacket.

Brother Miel's voice had an edge to it when he advised, "I will be direct; quit this place tomorrow at first light. The Robles family is in disarray, but such is the human condition. My fear is that quarreling among themselves will become something uglier, and I use this word because it is the most apt... bloodier."

Mort nodded, studying the bearded man's face. He meant every word.

"What is the problem with this family?" Mort asked.

Brother Miel sighed, "A story that is old and is destined to repeat itself. Don Robles fell madly in love with Maria Elena, who is younger than any of his adult children. His offspring thought their father secured a young nursemaid to care for him in his later years. The first ripple of discontent came when she declared she was pregnant."

Mort smiled sardonically, "I think I can guess where this is leading."

"Don Robles threw everyone into an uproar when he amended his will leaving Rancho Margarita to his recent bride and their unborn child. He left the other two ranches to his sons, who coincidentally only have daughters. However this is the most profitable and largest of the three. Don Robles would not hear any criticism of his wife."

"And now the old man has died, so there is no chance of changing his mind." Mort stated drily.

"Yes, but a few weeks prior to his death, Maria Elena Robles declared she'd lost the child, and then within a day of burying her husband, she claimed she is once more pregnant."

Mort crossed his arms. "I take it this is where the rub is to be found."

The friar shrugged his broad shoulders. "Yes for two reasons. One there has always been a doubt that Don Robles could engender a child. He was elderly and within the last year of his life his health declined. The second reason is there are rumors she has been using the ranch's *capataz*, the overseer as her stud."

"Well, the truth will out in about nine months."

"If it were that simple," Brother Miel said, "but Marco Robles is enamored of his stepmother, however there is quite a significant problem since he is already married."

Mort squinted and from a distance saw a tall, broad shouldered man studying him and the friar from afar. He was muscular and carried himself with a swagger missing from the other men milling about. Without being told he knew this was the overseer.

"You hinted this situation could become uglier, how so?" Mort asked.

13

The monk rubbed his face, and Mort could tell he was searching for the right words. "I have accompanied Padre Salazar since Mr. Kydd summoned me to Belize City as his traveling companion. I have walked the breadth of this land for many years, and I have witnessed the kindness and the cruelty that humans are capable of, however I have never found myself so close to bizarre incidents where people die horrifically. And it all started when I set my feet on the road close to whatever exists in the pouch that Father Salazar carries with him. This is no exaggeration coming from someone who has fought in wars."

"Has the violence been directed against either of you?"

"No, never, on the contrary. If anyone hinted any threat against us, they would suffer some horrible accident, which resulted in their death or severe injury. Horses would spook and trample them, a branch would inexplicably break from a tree and pin the person to the ground, and so forth. It took me a few days to detect this pattern. Once a person died, then the incidents would cease for at least two days. Horrible nightmares of the bloodiest battles I had fought in would stop, only to recommence a few days later."

"Did Father Salazar have the same experience?"

"No, strangely he did not." Brother Miel stated in a quiet voice. "But I know what he carries burdens his spirit."

"I wonder why Charles Kydd chose him."

"I do not know, but I suspect you can find the explanation in the letters Mr. Kydd wrote."

Mort was about to turn away when Brother Miel held him back by the arm. "This thing incites brutality Mort. Not just violence, but bloodlust, which I fear will agitate the turbulence in this family. They could turn against each other or any of us the longer we stay here."

14

Mort regarded the man. "I already decided to leave tomorrow, but I will heed your words and make sure we put distance between us and Rancho Las Margaritas as early as possible."

The friar nodded in agreement, "You know I will head back into Mexico before the cock crows. I will make my way to the Church of San Miguel Arcángel, in Ixmiquilpan. So I offer my goodbyes now."

"As do I, but tell me how you know so much about the Robles family?"

"Mort, I've learned through experience and observation that information is invaluable, especially if you wish to live a long and healthy life. I knew Rancho Las Margaritas would be the meeting place in California, and I would not come here blindly."

The men shook hands and went to their quarters. A few hours later they gathered to enjoy a sumptuous meal with the family. Mort noticed how Maria Elena Robles' eyes lingered on the satchel that Father Salazar brought with him to the gathering.

During the evening she casually asked about the contents, and he answered in a solemn voice, "It is a relic Doña Robles, of interest only for scholars of the Church."

After the meal Mort joined Marco Robles outside as they smoked a cigar. He heard about the ranch's cattle and sheep business, and the plans he had for the quarter horses they bred. Mort listened but also made note of where the outbuildings lay from the principal house.

Well after midnight Mort saw the door of his room inch open. Maria Elena Robles crept in, with a diaphanous wrapper draped over her night gown. Her thick hair hung to her waist. She walked to his bedside and stared down at him. Then with a fluid movement she shed her clothing and climbed on top of him. He'd expected this visit from the first time their eyes met.

15

Mort gave the youthful woman once married to an old man what she desired the most. He used her body for gratification with no sign of affection or intimacy beyond what passed between their bodies. She responded in kind. Perhaps the rumors she brought the *capataz* to her bed were only that, rumors. She was young, but he recognized the intelligence and ambition that shone in her eyes. It was doubtful she would give an overseer the power of claiming he fathered the heir to Las Margaritas, especially with a stepson who couldn't decide whether he hated or loved her more.

Sweat was still cooling on their skin when she offhandedly asked him about the reason he accompanied the old priest. Mort stifled the chuckle that rose in his chest. The question ended the illusion that she was only a sex-starved woman looking for pleasure and possibly someone to plant a child in her belly.

He gave her the same answer Padre Salazar gave when she asked during the meal. Mort then pulled her roughly under him and stopped any further questions by making it obvious he was not done with her for the night.

Dawn was tingeing the horizon when Mort washed himself and pulled a fresh set of clothing from a saddlebag sitting in a chair. The woman slipped from the room after he fell asleep. He already forewarned the old priest that he would come for him very early in the morning. He tapped on his door only once and the old man stepped outside, ready to leave.

They walked to the stables. Mort saddled not only Zabuca but a gelding he bought from Marco Robles the evening before. He also negotiated a saddle into the bargain.

The young servant with the glossy braids watched from the courtyard as the two riders cantered briskly away from Las Margaritas. As instructed by her mistress, she found the overseer and told him what she saw.

3.   Until the Morning

So why was the overseer from Las Margaritas following him and Father Salazar? Mort knew he acted under orders from Maria Elena Robles, and what would a wealthy widow want with a relic of the Catholic Church? For all she knew it was just a sliver of bone, or a scrap of clothing. It appeared she knew more than him.

He remembered the day Ema returned from a trip to Santa Barbara where she went to collect a message sent to her via carrier pigeon. She sent him off on this mission the next day. She only told him it was a relic, but never specified it belonged to the Church.

Her only warning had been, "Mort, I'm not sure myself what this is, however do not trust anyone who has been close to it. Guard your back." Ema then handed him the saddlebag with powerful sigils burned into the leather.

* * *

Noting that the winds died down, Mort closed his eyes and dozed, hoping that the weather would improve by the time they left the sanctuary of the miner's cabin. Father Salazar still snored in contented slumber.

Time slipped away, and he fell asleep. He sat up, and something told him dawn was not far off. Only embers remained of the fire. He reached over and shook out his boots to make sure nothing crawled in there. He holstered his six-shooter and unbarred the door. Outside all was quiet, the stars still shone, and the wind had dissipated.

The horizon turned yellow. Mort thought of the route he planned to take which was the Old Camino Real along the coastline. Originally established by Spain the missions started in San Diego and would take him to San Francisco. But with a party of men trailing behind them, he needed to rethink this plan.

Padre Salazar came to stand next to him. "Where to now Mr. Peccatum? Will those men be waiting for us?"

"Probably, but right now they don't know where we are."

Mort thought perhaps there was no need to go tearing off on the trail. He surveyed the area around him and saw the cabin was well hidden and difficult to find. No one could approach the shanty on the narrow trail without being seen.

The men ate beef jerky and hard crusts of bread. They drank water from the creek. Mort gave the horses feed he took from the stable and made sure they had water to drink. The sun was high overhead when Mort saddled them. Just as he finished the priest came out holding an old tin can.

"Mr. Peccatum, I believe this belongs to whoever lived here. It's a claim for the land, and the person's last will. It was behind the logs."

Mort pulled out one of the rolled pages dated six years before. The will written in a neat hand bore the signature of two witnesses and the testator was Jack Fletcher. When he read the name, a shiver ran through his body, and he could feel an unseen hand on his shoulder. He rolled and pushed the paper back into the coffee tin.

"I will make sure it gets to the right hands."

Mort and the old man retraced their steps, crossed the creek, and this is when they heard the murmur of voices of a sizeable group of people. From the treeline they saw them gathered around the tavern. A bedraggled lot, some were crying, and many nursed injuries.

None were the four men which had followed them.

The smell of smoke from different small fires drifted across the field surrounding the inn. Mort and the priest dismounted, walking among them until they found the tavern keeper. He stood watching a large fire where food was being prepared. They set another area up as a triage where the injured were lying on the ground.

Mort came up to the man, who seemed overwhelmed with all the surrounding disarray.

"What happened?" Mort questioned him.

The man's eyes widened when he saw Mort. "You, you're alive!"

"Obviously."

"I thought you were dead."

"Why would you think this?"

"When you and the old priest disappeared, I thought you continued down to Henricksville. Those men that came in after you, thought the same. They broke down the door to the room and rode off into the night when they found you were both gone."

Mort gestured around him, "And this?"

"A mudslide, it took the town out. It came out of nowhere. There are so many dead, but they're buried under debris. Where did you go?"

"To this old cabin up the trail. Looks like it's been deserted for years."

"Old Man Fletcher's cabin?"

"Probably, like I said it was empty."

The innkeeper passed his hand through his hair. "You know how many people have been lookin' for that place for the last few years? Everyone knows it's up there, but no one can find it."

"Just lucky then."

"Luck? That's an understatement. Everyone's hoping to find the map leading to the mine he owns."

Mort kept his face impassive. "So what happened to this man Fletcher?"

19

"Disappeared, everyone thinks they kilt' him. Rumor was he hit a mother lode of gold. They've kilt' men for less than that. Guess those stories about Fletcher's Curse is true after all."

Padre Salazar came to stand by Mort and listened to the innkeeper's words.

"What are the stories?"

"That Fletcher wanted his daughter back East to have his property, and anyone who goes looking for his place, either can't find it or takes a tumble off the side of the mountain. Seems like a fog bank just drifts in out of nowhere. And now this Mr. Henrick was fighting for the courts to declare Fletcher officially dead so he could buy the land, but he doesn't have to worry about that no more."

"Why not?" Mort asked him.

"Because he and his town got buried. Well, to be precise he didn't actually get buried, I heard from someone who saw it with his own two eyes, a piece of debris came crashing down and cut his head clear off."

"Your place seems to be the only one left standing."

"Yeah, everyone skedaddled out of here when that weird wind started blowing through. As you can see there's no room for you here, but take the old Cottonwood trail that skirts this canyon, and you'll avoid that mess down there."

Mort reached into his pocket and drew out a gold coin. "What's your name?"

"Arthur Periwinkle."

"Arthur, this is a little something, in case those men show up looking for us again. All you have to say… "

"Is that I never saw you again?" The man finished the sentence for him. "You've got my word on it. Those bastards tore up my place good looking for you fellas."

20

Then Arthur's eyes focused on a point behind Mort, "Hey you're letting the fire get too hot!" He walked off to a young man tending a fire where water was being boiled inside a cauldron.

Both men walked towards the tethered horses. Then an old woman toddled to Father Salazar, kneeled and grabbed him by the legs.

"Padre, bless me. He is coming for me, I saw him. Others have seen him."

The priest tried hard not to topple over. He placed his hand on the woman's bent head and made the sign of the cross over her.

"What did you see?" Mort asked the woman. Her eyes were bewildered as she looked up at the tall man dressed all in black like an undertaker.

"It was Death," she whispered, "a huge skeleton that beat its wings and caused the rain and wind to bring the mountain down on us. It laughed as people perished."

Father Salazar disengaged himself from the woman's grasp. Mort walked away and the old man followed him, his eyes wandering around to the people huddled in groups.

When they reached the horses, Mort saw Zabuca prancing around with ears laid back flat. She lunged against the reins that held her in place. He patted the horse on the neck and spoke to her in low tones then his hand brushed the saddlebag with the artifact in it. It was burning hot. He pulled it off the saddle. Immediately the horse quieted.

Father Salazar said in a quavering voice, "Perhaps I should carry it with me like before. Just take it out of there and put it in my bag."

Mort looked at the priest, and intoned in a deep voice, "*Daemonium tuam.*"

Father Salazar's eyes closed and then his eyelids twitched. He stood erect, threw back his head but his extremities jerked, and

21

drool dripped from the corner of his mouth. His monk's robe fluttered around him as his body spasmed.

Mort took off the glove on his right hand, placed it on the side of the man's neck and said, *"Exsolvo."*

The old man belched loudly, an odor of day old garbage surrounded him and then dissipated. He blinked, stopped all movement and looked at Mort with questioning eyes.

"What happened?"

Mort looked him up and down. "I will explain later, however you are not to carry the artifact again. Do you understand?"

He nodded uncertainly. Mort touched the saddlebag. Now it was ice cold.

He went to the other pack and pulled out a fifth of AA whiskey. He swallowed a long gulp. Now he understood Ema's warning to watch his back.

* * *

Several hours later Mort and Father Salazar guided their horses through the sage-lined Cottonwood trail. An occasional far off cloud streaked the blue sky. They stopped to drink water from their canteen. In the distance, a purplish range of hills loomed. They pushed on, the horses plodding steadily and it was Mort who would check behind them for signs they were not being followed. What he feared was that one of those riders was a tracker and a hunter, and he would not assume they perished in the mudslide.

The wind became cooler and the darkness of the mountain loomed above. Somewhere in the rocks a kit fox yapped. Mort found a small cove along a wall of rock. Bees buzzed around a spring at the entrance to a small cave. They made camp and Father Salazar who remained silent throughout the day, set a small fire and made coffee.

THE PATH TO PURGATORY

The horses with sweat-streaked flanks followed Mort like obedient children. He rubbed them down and gave them water. Then he returned to the fireside where he placed the saddles and the bags against an enormous boulder. He checked his rifle and then his Colt revolver. He passed the priest a piece of jerked beef to chew on.

When night settled upon the land Mort hid in the shadows, where the crackle of the fire would not drown out any stealthy sounds of anyone sneaking up on them. He prowled around with his Henry rifle, and just stood listening. It was only when he did not detect any noise of horse or man that he returned to stretch out by the orange embers.

It wasn't a noise that woke Mort, it was its absence. Even Father Salazar slept on his side in silence. Then his eyes focused on the kneeling figure across the fire from him. Etched against the velvet indigo of the night, the Indian woman watched him with an impassive expression on her face. A wide necklace of green stone beads and shell ornaments hung around her throat and covered her bare chest. A blue plumed headdress crowned her head. Then something tall moved in the darkness behind her. A withered, skeletal arm with elongated fingers helped her to stand. It towered over her, and he saw a cadaverous face that looked both human and animalistic, with many-pronged deer antlers rising from its forehead. Then they transmuted into rounded ram's horns. Tears tracked down her face as the snarling of a predatory cat vibrated in the air filling the moment with menace.

The creature wrapped its long leathery fingers around her throat. Her skin and the whites of her eyes yellowed. Blood spurted from her nose and tear ducts. Black vomit frothed from her mouth and covered her chin. She said only one word, *"xekik"*.

The creature communicated its message to Mort, "Generous rewards for those who serve me and punishment in equal measure for renegers. My will be done either in acquiescence or in fury."

The woman writhed in agony, and then she slowly changed, and Mort felt his heart thump hard in his chest, as she became a man, and the face that now contorted belonged to his brother Wilhelm who died twenty years ago. The yellow fever killed him. Mort felt anguish and deep sorrow twist in his being like a stiletto dagger. Then he awoke, and the sun shone full on his face.

Father Salazar crouched next to the fire stirring the coffee pot. "Nightmare, Mr. Peccatum?" he asked.

Mort wiped the sweat from his face, the intensity of the dream still wrapped around him. He stood up and dusted himself off. "Stop calling me Mr. Peccatum. Mort is fine."

The priest handed him a tin cup full of steaming coffee. "Well Mort, you were not the only one that saw it."

Mort stared off into the distance as he planned their journey, "Yes, Brother Miel told me he suffered from bad dreams..." The tall man stopped speaking and turned to stare at the priest who sipped from his cup. "Saw it?"

"Yes a nightmare creature, but not a nightmare, because I saw it too."

4.   Those Who Owe Heaven

The shop occupied the southeast corner of Clay and Kearney
Streets in San Francisco. The sign on the window display read E. St.
George, Druggist and Apothecary. Drugs, toilet articles, perfumes,
patent medicines and the choicest cigars lined the shelves or glass
cases displayed the more exquisite items. They were the finest
quality and overpriced, which is why its regular customers were
those who were not concerned with price but with quality. There
were other commodities unadvertised, but highly sought after.
Clientele came because they guaranteed anonymity and discretion;
therefore despite its unembellished appearance business was never
lacking.

Most clients came once and then requested to have future orders
delivered to them. However on their first visit a white-haired
gentleman with a silver mustache and mutton chops attended
them. His appearance was as impeccable as the goods he sold. He
wore a dark-clothed double-breasted coat unbuttoned over a silk
vest. He never wore the same tie. There was an ageless quality
about him and his accent was hard to place. By way of
introduction he told them, "My name is Miguel Angel; do not
hesitate to ask for my help."

No one ever saw him enter or leave the shop, and most assumed
he lived on the premises.

The most lucrative trade though took place upstairs on the
second floor. This is where apothecaries, druggists, physicians and
chemists came to buy rare and unheard of plants and herbs.
Mystics, occultists and those who dabbled in esoteric matters

occasionally walked up the narrow stairs to the richly furnished shop. Some never left.

An antique Persian rug covered the floor, casting a tangerine reflection to the light emanating from the fireplace. Seraphine Van Alstyne from New York sat on a mahogany gossip bench in the third-floor apartment above the shop. The sixty-year-old woman's name was once Seraphine Holbet until her marriage forty years before. A spotted, rat terrier type dog sat on her lap. Across from her sat a red-haired woman dressed in a high-collared gown of deepest Prussian blue.

"What was the message again?" the woman asked Seraphine.

"That you always honor your debts, and that you also help those who owe Heaven."

"And who is this supposed to help?"

"The man would not specify, but he said you would understand in time. That it's a matter of expiation of a sin."

"That really narrows it down." The woman named Ema said with a resigned sigh.

"The man explained this was the reason it should be me to come and see you. My parents owed you a great debt."

"What is the name of this man?"

"Alain Beaupre."

Ema stared at the woman in silence. "Very well, what should I call it?"

"Gigi."

The dog cocked her head at hearing her name. With a wag of her short tail, she jumped off Seraphine's lap and ran to Ema, leaping to sit next to her.

While they enjoyed tea and pastries, Seraphine stole glances at the beautiful woman who looked like she could be only thirty-five years old. She couldn't understand how her parents, who left New

Orleans in 1798, knew her when she lived there and went by the name of Madame Duplessis.

The white-haired man with the kind but enigmatic eyes started talking to the little dog. He said, "Ma belle, we meet again. Come with me I have a little treat for you downstairs." Gigi followed him happily, her stumpy tail wagging with enthusiasm.

Upon their parting, Ema extended her hands and thanked her, then whispered, almost as an afterthought, "Should anyone in your family ever need my help, they only need to send word here."

Inside the carriage, Seraphine pondered upon this strange encounter, wondering if this had anything to do with the letters her parent's solicitors told her they had waiting for her when she returned.

* * *

Ema sat by the fire, the flames licking low behind the grate. The little spotted dog lay across her thighs like a furry blanket. She snuffled and twitched her paws chasing a quarry in her dreams. In a moment Gigi awoke and pricked up her ears. Not long after a soft tap sounded at the front door of the shop.

Midnight had not arrived yet, and as if expecting this moment she had not changed from her daytime clothing. Ema descended the oak staircase, with a soft voice telling the little dog who whined to accompany her, "Stay." It obediently sat at the top step.

She threaded her way through the darkened first floor of the shop. A case clock ticked in the gloom, and with no hesitation to check who it was she unlocked the door opening it wide.

A Chinese man dressed in a mandarin collar robe and a red gold-stitched cap bowed to Ema. Beside him stood a young police officer. His face flushed when he saw her, "Ma'am begging your pardon, but we need your help, and he said you're the one that can do it." He pointed at the man standing next to him.

"Dr. Foo, please come in." Ema opened the door wider and let both men enter.

She turned in the dark and lit a lantern on a nearby table. The flame caught the wick, and a circle of light illuminated the group.

"How can I help you?" Ema asked Dr. Foo.

The man ran an apothecary shop in Chinatown as well as being a skilled physician in Chinese medicine. They sometimes traded herbs and seeds that he imported from Asia. He would ask Ema to start the seedlings to grow, for he knew of no one who could coax life to erupt from soil like she did.

Dr. Foo came to America from the Guangdong province in China. In five years he became fluent in the English language, in another five years he owned a thriving business.

"Miss Ema, you recall the murder of the woman Lee Cheng close to my shop?"

Ema nodded. They found the victim with a gaping wound in her head caused by the sharp blade of a hatchet. The walls of the room were blood-splattered, and across her mouth a bloodied handprint testified as to the assailant's attempt to stifle her screams.

In a previous conversation, Dr. Foo confided to her certain details since he had been the woman's landlord, and murder was not good for business. Within a day after her burial new tenants moved in. They told him the first night they heard a tap at the door, followed by a man's voice begging admittance, followed by the sound of the door being opened, the hurried step of two men, a struggle and then silence. The tenants examined the room and found it as they left it when they retired to bed. They vacated the premises, and no other came to take the family's place. Then the neighboring houses would hear a reenactment of the crime, and the woman pleading for her life several times. The words then died in a gurgle.

"Her murderer remains undetected?" she asked him.

The man nodded his head. Then Ema looked at the officer who coughed slightly, "Ma'am my name is George Morris, and I'm hoping that what I will tell you don't sound like I'm ready for the loony bin, but I swear it's the truth. Dr. Foo said you'd believe me."

"Officer Morris, all I can say is that you will say nothing that will shock me."

"I was walking my patrol along Dupont Street, and I was getting close to that tenement building that burned down last week. Seven people died, a bunch of others got hurt because they jumped from the windows."

The man hesitated and glanced at Dr. Foo who nodded his head.

"Well I'm standing there at the corner, and I suddenly get this eerie feeling, and my skin prickles. It was quiet, and then I hear someone singing in this high quavery voice in Chinese. And I'm thinking nobody can be in there. It's a death trap. The charred floors are sagging, and you can even see some iron bedsteads hanging through holes burned in the floors. Then I see this little, old Chinese man come out from the shadows. His hands and face are blackened, and he's got this can under his arm. I called out to him, telling him to get out of there, and he's speaking in Chinese to me, then he disappeared. One moment he's there and then poof he's gone."

Dr. Foo continued the narrative, "I was there because I heard this same story from someone else, and I wanted to see if it was true. It is as he described. The old man is Charlie Fung, he sold newspapers in Chinatown. He was known for hiding his money in tin cans. He died in the fire."

"Why did you bring Officer Morris to tell me this story?"

"I wanted you to hear it from another person. Some think Chinese people are superstitious."

Ema looked in Dr. Foo's eyes, "But, you know I am not like most people."

She turned to the policeman, "Officer Morris, I have no doubt that what you saw is absolutely the truth," Ema said, "but now I must speak with Dr. Foo alone. If you ever see other disquieting things of this type, please come and see me."

Out of the darkness behind her, a silver-haired gentleman wearing a velvet smoking jacket materialized. The policeman stifled a yell.

The man opened the door and smiled. "My name is Miguel Angel; do not hesitate to ask for my help once you return to our shop. Good night Mr. Morris."

The officer stumbled in his haste to get outside. Once the door closed Miguel Angel disappeared into the gloom.

"Dr. Foo tell me what you fear."

"Miss Ema, you understand then. A vicious murder, a strange fire that killed several people, all very close to my shop. The ghosts of these people are evidence that there is black magic being worked against me."

"Possibly, but seek the help of someone in your community versed in combating this. You of all people know many magicians."

"That is precisely why I have come to you. I fear that whoever has a hand in this claims to be my friend, but envies my wealth. This is *Ku* magic."

"What do you want from me?" Ema asked him in a quiet voice.

"To help identify who this person is so I may defeat them. This is the reason I have come here now at this hour of the night. There is no one to witness that I have visited your shop."

Ema nodded her head. "There was a grand celebration in your shop about three months ago."

30

The man beamed, but then looked quizzically at Ema. "Yes, it was the occasion of my marriage. Just today I learned that my wife is pregnant. There is more reason than ever that I should increase my business. I will have sons to inherit it."

Ema looked at him with searching eyes. "Indeed you are a fortunate man. Where is she from?"

"Her father is a merchant in Deadwood, South Dakota. He brought her himself and is very pleased with the marriage. When I saw her I realized how lucky I am for she is exquisite."

Ema regarded him. "A pretty young wife that will give you a child within the first year of marriage; some would say that is more precious even than gold. There are many women in the brothels, but very few suitable to be wives."

Dr. Foo stroked his chin in thought. He murmured, "In my happiness I have become blind."

"Was there any other who competed with you for her?"

The man's lips thinned in anger, "Ling, he has a very profitable laundry, but that was three years ago. Her father agreed to accept my offer because I would wait until she was older to consummate the marriage."

"Dr. Foo, I have given you something to think about, but I propose the following, the murder, the fire are all distractions from the true target. Look for an unfamiliar person to purchase your food from and launder your clothing."

His face grew alarmed for in that moment he knew that if someone stole his wife, and then they stole his future. What better way to ruin him than to kill her?

Miguel Angel appeared once more by the door.

Dr. Foo bowed to Ema. "You have my gratitude, and I owe you a great debt."

"Good night Dr. Foo." The man left with hurried steps.

Ema looked at Miguel Angel, with almost a sad smile, "No divination, just a study in human nature."

"Something we are both familiar with, Sivylla."

He turned and extinguished the lantern.

5.   What The Cat Dragged In

The next night, fog crept in with furtive silence. Ema looked down from the third-story window of the building on Kearney Street. She tugged on her shirt sleeve, worn under the man's style coat she wore. She owned many beautiful gowns, but practicality dictated that she always had a separate wardrobe of men's clothing tailored for her. Gigi sat on the window seat next to her and stared down.

She observed two men watching the shop since sundown, and then they walked into the shadows of an alley between two buildings across the street. Earlier that day Soledad her housekeeper sent her a message she thought someone watched the two-story adobe house she shared with Mort on the outskirts of the city. Were they waiting for her or Mort?

She smiled when she saw why the men left. Officer Morris took their place across the street. She knew he was working up the nerve to come and see her. Ema tossed her long braid over her shoulder and swept a bowler hat on her head. She descended the stairs and opened the front door when the policeman was about to knock.

"Officer Morris, what a pleasure, I was about to take a stroll, would you care to accompany me?"

The young man gaped speechlessly as he saw her outfit, then he smiled, and responded, "Of course, Miss St. George."

"Call me Ema."

They stepped away, and he inquired, "Won't you be locking your door?"

"No need, no one will attempt to enter."

Officer Morris looked at her then back at the door and shrugged his shoulder.

Ema smiled at him encouragingly, "I knew you would come back to visit. I didn't mention it when Dr. Foo was there, but Charlie Fung is not the first ghost you've seen."

"No ma'am, I've been seeing unusual things like that since I was a child, but I've learned to keep quiet about it. Lots of people will say they don't believe in spooks, but they're plenty scared of them."

They strolled along their steps echoing against the walls. All the businesses were closed.

"Is that why you're not scared of this area that you patrol by yourself at night? The policemen usually walk in pairs."

Officer Morris looked into Ema's deep green eyes, trying to guess if she was mocking him. For a moment he considered telling her he never felt alone, but he kept quiet. They kept walking on in companionable silence. He did not realize that Ema saw the tall man dressed in chain-mail that walked behind him, runic tattoos covering his arms and an etched axe hanging from his belt. A powerful guardian and Ema expected that Officer Morris' life would be adventurous, whether or not he wanted it.

Suddenly a roar of orange flames erupted from a storefront, igniting the sky and crackling like dozens of firecrackers. It was a small shack, a gathering place for locals to eat and trade information. The woman that owned the establishment cooked enormous pots of food that would vary from day to day, but it was plentiful and cheap.

Ema and George ran towards it. She wondered if the owner lived in the back of the store like so many business owners did.

"That's Hazel's place," George Morris said, pulling out the truncheon he carried on his belt.

THE PATH TO PURGATORY

The fire consumed the little shack, and it crumbled. The neighbors poured out of the nearby buildings bringing buckets of water to throw on it for fear that it would spread to the surrounding building. Already there had been over a hundred fires in the city, many of them suspected of being arson. The fire department was only four years old and still disorganized. George helped form two lines to help keep pouring water on it.

A distance away the road climbed upwards and Ema heard shouts. She followed the angry voices and saw two figures kicking someone on the ground. With purposeful strides she hurried towards them, and when they saw her both men stopped. It took them a moment to realize she was a woman.

One of them separated himself and said, "Bitch, there's nothing for ya' to see here." Then looked back at the other man and smiled, "Unless you want we take you in that alley, and remind ya' you just a stupid woman. Be off with ya'."

The other one grinned. "Maybe she need a beaten like a man, there's much can be done once them trousers come off."

The woman they attacked lay on the ground and raised pleading eyes to Ema. As if sensing the men's attention was no longer on her she scuttled away.

The man closest to Ema charged her, but he was overconfident, expecting that she would turn and run away. Instead she stepped forward and ducked under his outstretched arm, hooking his ankle with her boot, and then shoved him hard from behind. She heard the crunch of his nose as his entire face took the impetus of the fall. He grunted and pushed himself to all four. Then Ema kicked him in the side of his head, he sprawled on his back and didn't move.

The other man stared at her incomprehensibly, then grinned exposing a space where his two front teeth should be. He smacked one fist into the palm of his other hand and walked forward, circling around but staying out of arm's reach. His smile faded, and

35

he eyed her warily. He noticed the woman's breath was even, and there was no hint of fear in her eyes. Preoccupied with Ema, he didn't hear when George Morris came up behind him and hit him hard with his police club on the back of the head. He staggered for a moment and then fell forward and lay still.

Officer Morris looked at the other man, and asked Ema, "You did that?"

She nodded and turned to the beaten woman who held her side and tried to stand. Ema took her arm and helped her up. She recognized her as Hazel, the woman who ran the restaurant which burned down. Now that she stood next to her, Ema saw that the eyes which stared at her through the strands of her disheveled hair glimmered with a reflective light, and her mouth which at first glance seemed swollen was transforming itself into a muzzle.

"Help me." Hazel whispered, the tips of fangs peeking out below her upper lip.

* * *

The hired carriage stopped in front of a two-storied, long adobe house. It was away from the wharf, up a hill and remote. A pair of lit lanterns hung outside the front entrance that opened on a verandah. Sycamore and oaks grew nearby. By the time Ema came to the door, it stood open and an old woman with graying hair and dark eyes, held aloft a lamp.

Ema helped Hazel walk in and told the woman to prepare a room. The gray-haired servant nodded, and they followed her. The only sound was a fountain gurgling water in the middle of a tiled inner courtyard.

She steered Hazel into a parlor and sat her on a richly appointed chaise lounge. The woman pulled the hair from her face. Her features were human, and there was only a light bruising around

36

an eyebrow, much less than one would expect for the severity of the beating she received.

Ema pulled her coat and gloves off and tossed them over a sofa nearby. "Hazel, why were those men beating you?"

"For a couple of days now they came by telling me if I was smart, I needed to close up shop."

"Why would sailors want you to go out of business?"

"I overhear many conversations, men talk while they eat a meal. But I know that if I ever start saying anything that'll be the end of my little eatery. I thought maybe it was that, but they were never clear about the reason."

Ema gazed at her. "How did you know I wouldn't run screaming when I saw your face?"

"Because you're her." Hazel stated quietly.

"Would you care to expand on that?"

"You know that I'm a…" her voice trailed off.

"A shapeshifter." Ema finished the statement for her, "Yes I do, a feline one."

The woman nodded and pulled her black hair behind her ear. "Sometimes I can be just a cat, like any other you see on the streets. There are many things you see when you're traipsing around this city. I've seen you."

"You have?"

"Yes, when you're hunting, and I've also seen what you hunt. I knew you wouldn't be scared."

"So I guess I saved them, instead of you?"

"There are times I must transform into what I am. Into my true size, hunt, bring down prey and eat. I am larger than a mountain lion, and I must get far away from where anyone can see me. That is where I was going when those men stopped me."

"Do you still need to roam tonight?" Ema asked in a quiet voice.

Tears welled in Hazel's eyes. "Yes I do. I've put it off for too long."

"Then let us resume this conversation later. Come back here when you are ready."

"I will return in two days." Impulsively Hazel hugged Ema and then stripped off her clothing. The transformation started with her eyes, then her teeth. She threw open a window and without a backward glance jumped out and disappeared into the night.

6. Blood Offering

Ema finished eating her breakfast, when she heard the tread of someone walking upstairs. The only other person in the house was Soledad who in that moment was taking the plates from the table. Both women's eyes met in silent understanding. Gigi who had been happily gnawing on a bone, whined and yipped. Ema shushed her and Soledad picked up the little dog.

When Ema reached the bottom of the stairs, she looked up and saw Hazel waiting for her. She stood wrapped in a bed covering from the room she left only a few hours before. Her mouth was ringed in blood.

"Why don't you wash up? I'll have Soledad bring you something to wear. I'll be waiting for you in the dining room." Ema said.

Hazel just nodded and returned to the room.

Ten minutes later, they sat across from each other sipping coffee.

"I thought you would be gone longer." Ema murmured.

"So did I, but I found something that I've never seen before."

"Tell me everything."

Hazel looked down into the black liquid inside the cup she was holding, translating everything her senses as a shapeshifter witnessed into words. Her voice was a little unsteady. "When I haven't gone into the wild for so long, it floods all my senses. I prowl around just enjoying it, becoming familiar with everything out there. I don't hunt yet, even though I come across prey that I could capture."

"But last night, once I was deep in the forest I smelled it right away. The smell of blood, lots of human blood. There was something dangerous in the air."

"Dangerous for humans or animals?" Ema asked her.

"For both."

"What did you find?"

"They cleared the area, perhaps one or two months ago, and left the shorn trunk of a large tree. Blood soaked the center. I think they used it as an altar of some type."

Ema gazed at her. "Anything else left behind?"

"Yes, bodies; four of them. All men, each hanging at the different directions from meat hooks, like the ones at the slaughterhouses. All were missing their heads. Two had their hands and feet cut off. One had his heart ripped out, and they had flayed the last one."

"Were these parts of them left somewhere?" Ema asked her.

"No, nothing was there. If they were anywhere in the forest, I would have smelled them. Whoever did that took the parts of those men with them."

Ema stood up and paced back and forth. "Please continue."

"I have found dead men in the forest before. They've either been killed by an animal, by other men, or their own hand. I have never seen this before. My mother's people are Ojibwe, by not burying these bodies their spirits cannot journey to a place of peace and happiness."

"Perhaps the purpose of the method used was to offer them as blood sacrifices."

"There was something else."

Ema looked at the dark-haired woman.

"No animals touched any of those bodies. I couldn't scent any that even crossed into the clearing. No tracks there, plenty around the perimeter. The odor of blood and putrefaction of even one body would attract predators within minutes of their death from miles around. But those carcasses were untouched."

Hazel pulled a flowered shawl tighter around her shoulders. "Ema, one of those men was a sailor and I know who he is."

"How?"

"The body had a tattoo of a clipper ship on his back along with the words 'Homeward Bound'. He'd been coming to eat at my place, and one day he showed it to me. He'd just gotten it because he sailed around Cape Horn on his last voyage. I am positive this is the same man."

"Hazel, do you know which ship he worked on?"

"Yes, it's the *Manitou*. He told me the ship was being sold. It belongs to a man named Lane Robinson, well known in San Francisco. He made it rich with a mine out of the Comstock Lode. Now he's building a mansion on Nob Hill. He got out of the shipping business to become a banker. The sailor, I think his name was Boyd, talked to men eating at my place looking for a new ship to sail on."

Soledad came to the dining room. With a solemn face she signaled to Ema to follow her.

"What's wrong?" Hazel asked.

Soledad signaled again more urgently. She didn't speak, out of choice and Ema knew this. With a swirl of the green taffeta tea gown she wore, Ema walked after her towards the back of the home where food was prepared.

Soledad took Ema by the hand and brought her to the edge of a window which afforded a view that showed the sea off to the west, over the shoulder of a hill that rose behind the house. She pointed, and Ema saw two men standing behind trees halfway up the slope. They stood in the shade of the branches overhead.

Ema turned to Soledad, "Are those the same ones that were watching the house before?" The woman nodded.

41

Hazel who had followed them said with a worried tone, "Do you think they're looking for me?"

"No they've been watching the house before you came here. I also had men outside my shop."

"What do you think they want?"

"That's what I intend to find out." Ema said with a note of finality.

7.　Watch the Shadows

Mort and Father Salazar rode up to a solitary two-story, brick house. Fronted by a dirt road, barren hills rose behind it. A white-washed adobe wall with cactus clumps huddled here and there against it surrounded the structure. Adjacent was an old San Diego cemetery known by its Spanish name of El Campo Santo.

Thomas Whaley, a merchant, lived there with his family, but the local government also used part of the building as a courthouse. Several men milled about, and it was one of these that Mort came to find.

He picked out the slim man with a full beard. Dressed in a suit with a bowler hat on his head, he looked the picture of a prosperous merchant. His name was James Lynch. Jimmy to his friends, Mort knew him for twenty years. They traveled on the same wagon train to California in 1851 on the Santa Fe Trail. Jimmy believed he would strike it rich in the gold fields, three years rolled by and that dream evaporated. One day he showed up in San Francisco looking for Mort, he was penniless and homeless.

Ema and Mort became silent partners, financing a small apothecary shop he opened in San Diego which was a backwater town, but people still needed medicine and to purchase little luxuries to ease their life, and so he prospered. Most of his supplies came to him from the shop in San Francisco, and he eventually opened a livery stable which he owned in its entirety in Old Town. As the population increased so did his business.

The day that Mort came looking for him, the population in the city numbered 2,500 souls, and like most merchants he was active in the daily activity of the government. Once he recognized Mort he greeted him with a firm handshake and a clap on the back.

Father Salazar went to the Immaculate Conception Church in Old Town close to the Whaley homestead which offered him accommodations.

Mort stabled the horses at the livery Jimmy owned, and from there both men walked to his shop. Two employees were busy attending customers. Business was excellent. He lived upstairs with his wife and three children who were visiting his mother-in-law in Los Angeles. Jimmy invited him to stay instead of going to a hotel. Mort agreed and after settling himself into the small bedroom where he would sleep, he took the opportunity to pull out the family's tin tub and bathe.

Later that evening while they dined he caught up on events with Jimmy. The city was abuzz with the upcoming grand opening of the Horton House, a new luxury hotel touted as the largest and finest one in California south of San Francisco.

The next day, Mort left the artifact hidden in a cupboard inside the room where he slept. He encircled it with sigils and herbs used as a barrier. On top of it he placed a silver crucifix, etched with intricate symbols. After he experienced that horrible nightmare, the relic became ice cold to the touch, even if the temperature outside was hot. He felt it became dormant, but he knew this was a temporary situation.

Outside a faint breeze stirred, and the air was pleasant and warm. Both men went to a local eatery for breakfast and feasted on beans, sourdough bread with honey and bacon. Strong, black coffee followed this. A mixed lot of Spanish men, merchants, frontiersmen and farmers crowded the place.

THE PATH TO PURGATORY

Once finished, Jimmy took Mort to see Horton House located on the northwest corner of Fourth and D Streets. The smell of animals, humans and perfumed clothing from the more affluent mingled in the midday heat, as everyone paraded around. In the crush of people, Mort saw what he hoped for and dreaded at the same time. It was the overseer from Las Margaritas, accompanied only by another man. He stepped behind a wide column and watched them. They scanned the crowds, and he knew they were looking for him. Eventually they would make it down to the church hoping to find the priest, and that's where they would find him.

Mort pulled Jimmy aside. "I have little time to explain, but I got two men following me, and I need to get some answers. Double back to the stable, and I will lead them there. Tell that old man you got working for you to cool his heels at the saloon."

Jimmy grinned, "That old son-of-a-bitch is meaner than a rattlesnake. He's not gonna wanna miss this."

Mort nodded and turned away. He was taller than most men, so he knew he was easy to pick out, but it couldn't appear obvious. The crowd flowed around him, and he hid next to a woman with a parasol. She walked towards where the men stood. At a precise moment he let her meander beyond him so he became visible, then caught up with her, and purposely bumped shoulders with a man heading in the opposite direction. This gave him a chance to glance behind, and he saw they both were on his trail.

Mort crossed over and made his way towards the livery stable. A cloud of dirt hung in the air kicked up by the wagons, carriages and horses that traversed through the principal thoroughfare. He knew they would wait until he was inside because they didn't want anyone to see what they planned for him.

He meandered like someone unaware he's being followed. As he did so, he felt a cold deep-burning anger that these men were hunting him and the priest over what they thought was a relic.

45

A squinty-eyed old man with a white droopy mustache covering his upper lip stood inside the livery. "Need your hoss saddled?" he asked Mort.

Both men walked in after Mort, and the next thing they knew Jimmy was pointing his rifle on them from behind and closed the livery door. Mort aimed his Colt revolver at the overseer's belly. He was a rough-looking character wearing a flat-brimmed hat and beat-up chaps. Deep-set eyes accented his heavily boned face that was topped by a shock of coarse black hair. The other man tried to step back until he felt the barrel of Jimmy's rifle poke him in the spine.

The old man cackled, "These two best mind their manners, 'cause I think this auger is itchin' to make them bite the ground with that black-eyed Susan."

Mort stepped up close to him and asked in a deceptively gentle voice, "Why have you been trailin' after me since we left Las Margaritas?"

The man puffed up his chest, and he stepped forward. Mort caught him by the front of his shirt and vest and hit him across the face with the butt of the revolver. Using the muzzle as a pointer, Mort said, "Next time it's the front end of this that's gonna talk for me."

Blood trickled from a cut on the man's cheekbone. He smiled, but Mort knew there was murder in it. "You'll not live to get to San Francisco," he said. "I'll see to that."

Mort then inspected him since he was up close, and he understood what was familiar about the man, "You're one of Don Robles' bastards, huh?"

He could tell that it was like someone had slapped him across the mouth, and it wasn't the first time he'd felt the sting of those words; he went white around the lips.

"So what did she promise you?" Mort asked.

"Doña Robles," Mort saw a look in the man's eyes that confirmed the black-haired witch had ensnared him deep and tight, "agreed to marry me. She needs a man to run Las Margaritas, otherwise her stepsons will run her off and keep it for themselves. Better married to a Robles bastard, then being sent to a convent where they'll shut her away so they can keep it all."

"But she has a Robles child in her belly, that's who will get Las Margaritas." Mort pointed out.

"She ain't got no baby, the best that old man could do was look at a naked woman, and you can't make a baby with your eyeballs. But I'll give her one right away, as soon as I get back, but she said only if I bring what you got."

"Do you know what it is?"

"Nah, just somethin' the priest has been draggin' through Mexico."

"So why would she want it so badly?" Mort asked an obvious question.

"She told me if she can bring a holy relic to the church down there, they'll marry us over any complaints the Robles will make. You know how much money that little chapel will make with a saint's tooth or whatever on the altar? Everyone looks out for their own, and I'll get mine."

Mort holstered his gun and pushed the man back. "What's your name?" he asked.

"Maximo Sandoval."

"Well Max you're going to your wedding night empty-handed."

The man's hands balled into fists. Mort could see that he knew Maria Elena Robles would not open her bedroom door or anything else unless he came back with this prize.

Mort stole a glance at the other man who was looking serious as all get out. He wondered if he knew that what he just overheard guaranteed he wouldn't make it back to Las Margaritas alive.

In contrast, a taunting smile spread across Sandoval's face, as he straightened up. He suddenly went for his gun, and Mort clouted him on the side of the face with a fist, catching him on the angle of his jaw.

Through gritted teeth Mort growled, "You stupid son-of-a-bitch you're being played by that widow-woman. She ain't gonna marry you no matter what you bring her. I got an excellent look at the birthmark she's got on the swell of her ass, *gratis*."

Maximo Sandoval stepped back and looked Mort up and down and stopped at his blue eyes. He could tell the tall man was not lying. Fury transformed his face and with an agile twist of his arm he pulled out a long knife hidden in a sheath behind his back.

Mort stepped back out of arm's reach. He didn't want to kill this man, but he might be forced to. He could tell Sandoval wasn't thinking anymore, the insanity of jealousy and disappointment blinded him.

It was then that the sound of fluttering wings filled the air as the pigeons roosting in the rafters scattered and even hit the wood of the roof to escape something that arrived in their space.

A low grunting howl filled the air, and all the men's eyes searched the murkiness of the loft above them. The horses in the stalls kicked at the wood and they pinned their ears back. They neighed and snorted.

The smell of rotting fruit and garbage enveloped them, and then all five sets of eyes widened when they saw the air quiver and shimmer transparently above the main beam of the ceiling. The howl echoed, and they saw a figure crouched there. A tail whipped furiously, and multiple arms moved apart from the hind legs which stretched out behind it. Eyes like twin red flames danced in its face.

"Jesus, Mary and Joseph!" James Lynch said in a voice filled with terror.

THE PATH TO PURGATORY

The thing launched itself downward, and the men scattered away, but there was only one of them it wanted. Its trajectory was swift and unerring towards Maximo Sandoval who stood paralyzed by fear.

It had a monstrously colossal head set on a short neck with a simian aspect to it. The jaws opened to display pointed yellow teeth that snapped with a crack on the man's neck. Four arms ended in black tipped claws and the feet ended in paws with curved talons. Two large-knuckled hands held the man secure by the shoulders while the other two disemboweled him. A quivering scream gurgled to a stop as his intestines spilled to the floor. The metallic smell of blood filled the space.

Mort pulled a long knife from a holster under his arm. Its silver glint glowed, and the etchings on it sparkled. He held Ema's dagger Iron Horse, and it vibrated in his grip. He plunged it into the creature's back and it roared horribly, filling the stable with its unearthly echo. He pulled it out, and the beast fell to the ground, turning rage-filled eyes to Mort as it howled its fury. Fangs dripped with saliva and the hackles rose on its back. Impotence filled its eyes, and Mort realized it could not attack him. Standing on its hind legs, it was as tall as an adult man. Shaking its black-furred mane, it roared then crouched and leaped onto the main truss of the ceiling where it dissolved into the murkiness.

8. Don't Shoot the Messenger

Mort sheathed the knife and called out for the other men. He found the old man in one stall hiding behind a horse. Jimmy wedged himself into a corner behind some barrels, and Sandoval's companion curled himself into a ball. He urinated and soiled himself. When Mort pulled him to his feet, he kept reciting Our Father in Spanish.

Jimmy came up to Mort, his face drenched in sweat. "What in the name of God was that?" The old man came up behind him, his eyes averted from the corpse of the man that still twitched.

Mort turned to the old man, "What's your name?"

"Ned."

"I want you to stand outside and turn away any customers. Tell them you had a horse go down, and you'll need a few hours to get it out of here."

Jimmy's voice still quavered, "Mort, what do you want me to do?"

"Get me some horse blankets so we can wrap up this body. Do you have a wagon where we can load it up?"

The man nodded and Mort could see he was glad to have a reason to leave. He came with blankets and helped place the body on it.

While he waited for Jimmy to return, he grabbed the other man who stood as if entranced watching Sandoval's wrapped body. "Where are the other two men?"

The man tore his eyes away, and he whispered, "They died in the mudslide. Sandoval sent them into the town to look for you and the priest."

"I suggest you go somewhere to change your clothing, get on your horse and head back to Las Margaritas today."

The man licked his lips nervously, nodded and slipped out the front door. Not long after Jimmy showed up with a narrow wagon which he backed into the double doors of the livery. They loaded up the body.

Ned turned to Jimmy, "I'll put some sawdust over the blood, and tidy up, but I ain't stayin' here overnight."

Mort turned to the old man, "It won't be back Ned."

"How d'you know that?"

"I just do."

"Well, all I know is I'm gonna sleep on a pew in some church in this town with a prayer book for a pillow."

Jimmy pulled the wagon forward and Mort climbed in next to him. Before Mort could ask he volunteered, "I know where we can take the body. There's a small cemetery on the edge of town where they bury vagrants. The sexton always has a couple of holes ready for bodies. You'd be surprised how many men die or get killed and we don't even know their name."

Mort nodded.

In an uncertain voice, Jimmy said, "I've seen my share of strange things, especially when Ema's around, but never like this. I think I'll have a hard time convincing Ned to keep working for me."

Mort looked askance at the man next to him, "Jimmy what if I told you that thing was trying to protect me."

The slim, bearded man stayed silent as the horse plodded down the dusty road. "Yeah, it appeared when that man pulled his knife out, but what is it?"

"Something from hell." Mort said. "Jimmy, I need to get to San Francisco quick."

"There's a steamer leaving tomorrow that'll get you there in two days."

51

They pulled in through sagging gates. Black chaparral dotted the deserted graveyard and most of the mounds were unmarked. In a weed-covered corner, an open grave had been dug, and between both men they dumped the body inside. Mort took a shovel Jimmy brought and buried it. He gave Jimmy money to have a priest come out and recite prayers over him and erect a wooden cross. He also gave him the horse the priest used and additional money to buy passage on the steamer. Then he explained he needed to check on Father Salazar.

Jimmy took him to the Church, and Mort stepped down and watched as the buckboard squeaked and rattled off down the road. He stepped into the dim interior that smelled faintly of incense. The monsignor recognized him, and with a worried look on his face approached him.

"Mr. Peccatum I am so glad you are here. There is a problem with Father Salazar."

The older man wiped his brow with a trembling hand.

"What has happened?"

"This morning he prepared to celebrate mass with me, and as he entered the church, he became very ill. We took him to a room where he could lie down, and afterwards he fell into a slumber that we could not wake him from. He thrashed about on the bed, and nothing we did could rouse him. Only a few minutes ago he awoke, but it seems something is not right with him. I am at a loss how to help him."

The priest hesitated, and then plunged on with what worried him, "I thought of calling a physician, but I think this is a spiritual matter. I have prayed all afternoon, and the only thing I know is that I must ask you to take Father Salazar away from here.

The older man looked away from Mort's steady gaze.

"I understand; can he stay overnight?"

THE PATH TO PURGATORY

The priest nodded, warring between what he knew was his Christian duty, and the illogical but pressing fear that he needed to get Father Salazar out from under their roof.

Mort pressed a coin into his hand and asked for someone to bring the priest to the wharf where the steamer would leave from in the morning.

Near to the church Mort walked into a telegraph office. He sent a brief message to Ema that only she would understand, explaining how and when he would arrive in San Francisco.

He then walked down to 5ᵗʰ Avenue, near to a newly constructed wharf. There were no trees or shrubs. Brown wooden structures, most of them unpainted were saloons and brothels ready to welcome sailors coming off the docked ships. Wagon wheels veined the dirt street. He stepped into one that seemed more upscale. An enforcer stood outside, making sure troublemakers didn't make it through the front door.

Mort went to a long, well polished mahogany bar and asked for a shot of their best whiskey. A mirror hung on the wall and he could see several cards games going on behind him. Other men disappeared upstairs, where the brothel was being run from, but there were no sailors or other rowdy types. A piano player in the corner filled the place with music, and he could see a great deal of money trading hands.

Mort pondered the contents of his saddlebag in Jimmy's cupboard. His realized his protection lay in the fact he was the one transporting it to San Francisco, and somehow it was using Father Salazar's psychic being to overrule the power of the runic symbols surrounding it. It had dispatched a guardian to make sure it reached its destination.

There was another presentiment he examined, which was that he was still being followed. He recalled the murdered passengers and overturned coach he found in the gulch, left as food for scavengers. Another interested party wanted to make sure he reached San Francisco, and they were using him to do the dirty work of transporting it, along with the risk of being murdered for his troubles.

Someone was watching, waiting and planning at his expense and the thing that bothered him was the way they clung to his trail. He thought of the moccasin prints and knew they brought someone along who could track him no matter how stealthy he wanted to be. He was betting they thought he would continue up the Old Camino Trail to San Francisco instead of taking the steamer. The only reason they had not taken it off his hands was because they knew how dangerous it was.

Mort signaled the bartender for another shot.

He hoped that sending Jimmy to purchase the tickets would throw them off. It bothered him he didn't know who was behind this. Maria Elena Robles and Sandoval motivated by greed were easy to understand. He wasn't sure how much the widow knew about what Father Salazar brought with him from British Honduras, but it outgunned Sandoval in the metaphysical world. Those weak sisters he brought with him, loyal to the *capataz* from Las Margaritas didn't stand a chance to survive from the moment they started their pursuit of him.

Mort rubbed the stubble on his jaw and looked at his reflection in the mirror. He saw a tall man with blonde hair, streaked almost white at the tips, with a mustache to match. Crow's feet were showing around his pale blue eyes. More than once he'd been accused of having the best poker face, absent of displeasure or happiness, regardless of what he was feeling.

There were other men at the bar, but there was enough space that none rubbed elbows unless they knew each other. A man came in and stood close to him, even though he had plenty of space on the other side. Mort glanced at the mirror and saw the men milling about look pointedly at the man, and they either left the place or walked off to the sides of the room.

Mort broke out into a wide grin, it didn't reach his eyes and anyone who knew him would have realized this was a dangerous thing.

"What's funny?" the balding man next to him growled. He had a thick body, and part of his cheek and neck exhibited burn scars that looked like melted wax. Mort guessed he had been in the vicinity of an explosion.

Mort centered his attention on the man, and confusedly said, "Huh?"

"What's so goddamn funny?" The man stepped in closer to Mort. He was just as tall.

"You," Mort said shortly, "damn you are one ugly son-of-a-bitch. I bet those whore upstairs charge you extra right?"

The man stared back, not used to having someone attack him about his looks. Somebody behind them chuckled, and spittle came from his lips as he raged, "Why, you...!"

Mort slapped him with an open palm across his mouth with enough force to jerk his head back. The man swung at him, a roar starting from the back of his throat, but Mort expected his reaction and calculated his reach. He stepped back, and once the fist whistled by his face, he walloped the man's body hard. The thick man didn't flinch, and he swung again and hit Mort in the head, who staggered back. The man hit him with a powerful right that sent him reeling back onto the floor. He followed up to kick him in the face, but Mort jerked aside and the boot caught him on the shoulder.

Rolling to get some distance from his attacker, Mort regained his feet, and when the man charged him he jabbed him with a left to the face that stopped him and smashed his lip into his teeth. Like a bull the man lowered his head and charged, but Mort sidestepped him and sent a right uppercut into his face that threw him against the bar. His ham fist closed around a bottle and he flung it across the room. Mort ducked and with the momentum dove in and grabbed the man about the knees crashing him to the floor. He head-butted him in the stomach and then he regained his feet.

The dazed man was slow to stand up, but before he could center himself, Mort slapped him hard across the face, and then punched him in the solar plexus. A groan escaped his lips when Mort hit him with a wicked left hook that spun him around. A right to the chin knocked him out, and he went down hard.

Without another word, Mort tossed a coin on the bar, stepped over the man and left the saloon.

9.   Cavalry on the Horizon

The moon was rising when Mort left Jimmy's shop. He kept to the shadows along the road, making him almost invisible in the darksome light. From his black, low-crowned hat to his somber clothing there was nothing to catch the glint of light. He stood momentarily in a pool of shadows and studied everything around him to make sure there were no eyes on him. He slid into a side door of the livery stable.

Zabuca whinnied when she smelled him. True to his word Ned was nowhere to be found, however everything inside was tidy. Mort stashed his saddlebags in a nondescript chest between the stalls. The one with the relic felt like a block of ice was inside it.

He wasn't sure if it was someone who saw him visit the telegraph office, or guessed that his friend was buying tickets for him on the steamboat, but he couldn't risk Jimmy's household if they came after him again.

He also had to consider that whoever was behind this might have enough pull with the law to have him arrested on some trumped-up charges. He felt this was the safest place to stay until he boarded the steamer.

Then his ears picked up the sound of rustling up in the rafters, and he stood up, all senses on alert. It sounded too big to be pigeons or any other small bird.

Then a low whistle sounded and he knew what perched above him. He whistled back, and the flap of large wings preceded a golden eagle that swooped down and perched on the edge of an empty stall. It cocked its head to one side and whistled again. The bird rustled its feathers and then flew up into the darkness above.

He found a thick blanket and spread it down in the stall next to Zabuca's stable. He pulled his hat over his eyes and slept. Ema had sent him a watchdog, albeit one with feathers instead of fur, but he knew of none more protective.

A cock crowed hoarsely in the predawn darkness, in response several dogs barked and then howled. A hunched figure shuffled in the yard outside of where the priests of the Immaculate Conception Church slept. It was an old woman dressed in black with a shawl over her head; she used a crooked staff to propel herself forward. She came to a small courtyard where an adobe oven was used to bake bread, and a wooden door led into the kitchen.

The woman scratched at the door and pushed hard but it wouldn't budge. She then pressed her face against the edge of where the door met the wall and sniffed audibly. She whined like an animal, and then the sound lowered and became a growl. The hump on her back became more pronounced, and she pressed her nose once again to the space between the door and the frame, like an animal hunting a quarry.

She stepped back and looked at the windows on either side. Her eyes shone like two wet, black stones in her pallid face. Suddenly the door opened wide, and a man stood there. His silver-colored hair hung to his shoulders, and white mutton-chop whiskers covered his cheeks.

"My name is Miguel Angel, can I help you?"

The hunchbacked figure spit and hissed. It scuttled backwards like a beetle.

The man asked in a soft voice, "Have we met before?"

The figure dropped to all four and made a clicking noise. A head popped forward like a turtle thrusting itself out of its shell on an elongated neck. It no longer looked human. It clicked threateningly and made as if to charge the figure at the door.

"Ah, I see we have." the man said. He swung a silver sword that winked brightly even in the opaque light and cut off the creature's head. It rolled towards the oven, and the body crumbled to the ground. The remains, both sections of it immolated themselves and a rancid stink drifted up with the column of smoke.

The man stepped back into the kitchen and closed the door.

10. Chasing Death

Ema opened the note delivered from Paul Kane assistant at Gray's Undertakers. He would contact Mort when something unusual came to them, and in his absence she received the missive. She knew there was more to this death than a mysterious suicide otherwise he would not have notified them.

> *They found the body of an unknown man hanging in a deserted house across the Slough, near the Fifth Street Bridge. It was very much decomposed. He was well dressed in black broadcloth, swallowtail coat, black felt hat, polished boots, and had evidently been hanging there for several weeks. I will provide further details in person. PK.*

She skimmed it, and gave the messenger who stood waiting a verbal reply, "Tell him tonight at dusk; at his place of employment."

* * *

The sun glowed dimly on the horizon when a front coupe carriage stopped in front of Gray's Undertaker on Sacramento Street. The driver stepped down from his perch and opened the carriage door. Diamond-pleated burgundy satin lined the interior, and he held a woman's gloved hand as she descended. Inside a little spotted dog stayed behind waiting patiently.

Paul Kane, a slim dark-haired man wearing wire spectacles opened the door and for the first time saw the face of Mort Peccatum's partner in the apothecary shop. She was lovely with her emerald eyes and reddish copper hair, piled under a hat of the latest fashion.

He made sure that he was the only one left in the building, which was easy since none of the employees wanted to be under its roof once the sun set. They witnessed too many unusual noises and shadows.

Paul Kane brought Ema to a small parlor. "Mort is away taking care of business, and he asked me to come in his stead if we received any message from you."

Miss… " Paul stopped wondering what to call her.

"Call me Ema. Tell me about the body found hanging in the deserted house."

"The coroner went to where they found it, and without proof of an injury they determined it to be a suicide, and sent the remains directly to us. They made a cursory check of the pockets and found nothing, but I discovered something inside the inner lining of the coat."

"Show me what you found."

Paul brought out a box and opened it. Inside was a newspaper cutting, and next to it what appeared to be small chips of ivory. Upon closer inspection, Ema found them to be children's teeth. Based on their size, they came from different-aged children. Not all were milk teeth.

The content of the article was:

Missouri
March 21, 1870
The affair occurred at the farmhouse of Otto Bauer. An entire family, comprising five persons, were discovered weltering in their

blood, late yesterday afternoon, by one neighbor, who called at the house. The middle-aged farmer was found with his throat cut from ear to ear as was his son. His throat was horribly gashed in such a manner as to almost sever the head from the body. His son's wife had her skull fearfully crushed as if by an axe, but her throat had also been slashed beforehand. Two children, aged respectively eight months and three years, had been dispatched in the same manner as the mother. All the bodies were stiff when found and the supposition is that the murder was committed the night before the discovery. The sheriff found someone had stolen some money, but they left many items of value and jewelry behind. The coroner also found that both children had all their teeth pulled from their head. The family was not known to have any enemies.

Ema looked up at Paul. "Did you find anything else?" she asked him.

"There is nothing to confirm his identity. However, there is a tattoo and what appears to be a brand on certain parts of his body." The undertaker studied the woman, expecting her to recoil in distaste, instead she said, "Show me."

"Ema, skin on bones is all that's left. It is not a pleasant sight."

She smiled at him. "Paul, I promise I will not have a case of the vapors. It is important that I see exactly what is on him."

"Then follow me." He took a lantern from the table and lit their way down a long corridor to the back of the building, and then into a room which held an unpleasant odor. She knew that it could be worse if more bodies awaited burial.

Paul went to a slab and pulled back the blanket. Desiccated skin clung to a skeletonized man's figure. The worst smell coming from it had come and gone during the first days when its innards putrefied and leaked downwards around it. The undertaker pointed to a tattoo on the man's chest over where his heart would be. It was a P with an S superimposed over it in an intricate calligraphy style, which ended in a teardrop shape, filled in red ink similar to a drop of blood.

Ema nodded, and said, "Where is the brand?"

Paul licked his lips and hesitated. "Ema there is something else besides the brand, and I don't understand what it is. I've seen nothing like it."

She stared into his eyes. She could tell that he was more than perplexed by it, he was frightened. "Then perhaps together we can figure out what it is."

"Very well, I need to turn him over."

"I will help you." Between both of them they turned it over. The remains did not weigh much. At the base of the spine, branded into the skin at the base of his spine was the same image. Ema examined it and saw that it was a recent burn. Then she looked above it and saw what disturbed Paul. There was a bony extension coiled around the vertebrae that broke through the dried out flesh. It looked like a scorpion's tail that ended with the stinger at the base of his neck.

They covered the body. He turned to her and asked, "Ema have you seen this before?"

Ema knew he meant everything from the tattoo to the hidden scorpion tail inside the man's body. "Paul, how much do you want to know?"

He was about to answer, when he hesitated, realizing what she meant by her question. Once she told him, he could not hide inside the safety of ignorance.

"Tell me everything."

Ema studied him for a moment. "I will give you a warning before I tell you what you ask. Pretend ignorance because your life will depend on this, and this means you can never share it with anyone else."

"Why?"

"Because knowledge of the symbol and what this man became is a well guarded secret by powerful people. It has been thus for hundreds of years, perhaps longer."

He nodded, "I understand." The man looked at Ema expectantly, and she thought, "I hope that it is everything you want, because I know it will be everything you fear in your nightmares." However she acknowledged to herself that he was a good source of information, and he was very closed-mouthed. His survival would depend on this.

"This insignia stands for the Order of Primus Sanguis. The Order of First Blood. They are Bloodletters."

"You mean like when doctors use leeches on you?" In his youth, Paul dreamed of becoming a physician, but his family was poor and like others he sought his fortune on the west coast.

"I will give you an abbreviated answer. Those who belong to this order hide behind the procedure of bloodletting. This practice has fallen out of favor in current times, but for thousands of years they did it to combat illness. The Catholic Church prohibited this method starting in the 11th century. They got a little carried away and forbade clergy and even lower monks from practicing medicine. By 1247, they outlawed all burning and cutting which meant surgery or in this case bloodletting, based on the principle that the Church shunned bloodshed."

Paul looked at her, and replied uncertainly, "Doesn't sound too bad of a reason."

"The Church gets a lot of things wrong, but this one they were right about, their error was to prohibit the clergy from practicing medicine in its entirety. Bloodletters who belonged to this order concealed their actions behind helping the sick. Their true purpose was to spill blood in enormous quantities when evil practices require it."

Paul Kane felt his gut churn. Understanding dawned on him. He thought of the newspaper cutting and the children's teeth. He realized this man spilled blood in one way or another.

"Ema, there was a murder that occurred two months ago, which I think is tied to this."

"Describe everything you know about it."

"Someone raped and murdered a child by the name of Maggie Ryan. They found her body underneath the wharf by Drumm and Pacific Streets."

"Yes, I read the story in the newspapers."

"They accused Charles Quinn, and he pled insanity at his trial. His brother came and testified he suffered several blows to his head in his youth. He received life in prison, even though there was a fear the crowd would drag him from the cell and hang him. From the beginning there were whispers that he confessed to a crime he didn't commit. Lockhart and O'Brien, were the undertakers who handled the girl's body. I used to work there and still have friends who describe unusual cases. One of them told me the Ryan girl was missing all her teeth. She was seven years old, and they thought it a curious thing. Quinn never confessed doing that to her."

"You think this man was the one that killed Maggie Ryan?"

Paul Kane looked at Ema with troubled eyes and nodded.

"Lockhart usually caters to a more upscale clientele, why didn't Grays handle the girl's body?"

"Mrs. Ryan, the child's mother, works for one of the wealthiest citizens of San Francisco. She is a servant in his house, and he paid for all the arrangements."

"Do you know his name?" Ema asked.

"Yes I do, but I was asked to keep it in confidence since the man preferred to remain anonymous."

"I find modesty in these types of individuals to be rare." Ema commented drily.

"His name is Lane Robinson."

Ema thought of her conversation with Hazel.

"Perhaps this man sought his own destruction because the perversity of his actions finally overwhelmed his conscience." The undertaker continued in a questioning tone.

"Paul would you estimate this man died around the time of Charles Quinn's trial?" Ema asked him.

"Yes, very close in time."

"Then perhaps he did not die by his own hand. You described he was well dressed, so obviously he was not unemployed or homeless."

Paul raised his eyebrows and paced back and forth. He came back to stand next to the draped slab.

"Yes, his outfit cost a pretty penny. His clothes would have cost a day laborer a month's wages."

The man hesitated a moment, "I thought perhaps the deformity in his back was causing him pain and he did away with himself because of it."

"Paul, it is not a deformity." The statement hung in the air between them. Shadows cast by the lantern danced across the walls.

"What else can it be?"

Ema understood his mind decided this was the sanest explanation.

"When was he found?"

"Yesterday evening, they brought him in this morning."

"Who knows that he is here?

Ema measured her words because she knew that for all his open-mindedness and curiosity, he would balk at what she was about to say.

"The coroner, he probably mentioned it to a newspaperman at the Chronicle. I hate to say it, but a man's suicide is commonplace in this city."

"Who discovered the body?"

"A worker examining properties where the proposed Second Street Cut is to take place. The plan is to demolish any buildings standing in the vicinity. The fear is that some homeless were living there, not all of them sleep under the wharves."

"So, this man's death could have gone undiscovered, one could almost say this was the hoped for conclusion."

"Perhaps," he murmured, "but Ema you said this growth is not a deformity."

"No, he grew it." She stated simply.

Paul Kane looked at her in dumbfounded silence.

Ema gazed into the gloom that filled the corners of the room. She could feel the stare of the dead who didn't know about or accept their deaths. Then in unison they all looked towards the door.

Both of them heard the noise that echoed softly down the corridor leading to the room where they waited at.

In answer to her unspoken question, he said, "There is no one else in the building, and I am expecting no visitors."

"They're here for it." She motioned to the draped slab.

The sound of footsteps came closer.

"Well, they can have it." Paul said with finality.

"They will leave no witnesses behind who have seen this man's body without clothing."

Paul felt his mouth grow dry. "Ema, I am sorry I didn't mean to put you in peril. I thought Mort would be the one to come. Perhaps if we explain to whoever is there that we just think it's a simple suicide. You came to view the body because someone you know is missing."

Ema looked at him with kind eyes, knowing he did not understand how serious this situation was. "This sounds like a convincing story. Let's relate this to them, and see what happens, but even if it was the truth, I doubt they would accept it."

He nodded hesitantly and then they heard the footsteps stop at the door. Ema pulled out a handkerchief, and it held it to her face. She then winked at Paul, and he just stared back at her with an open mouth.

"Mr. Kane, please tell me this is not my fiancée." She sobbed quietly.

The door swung open, and two men stood there. They were both muscled and bore a military air.

"Gentlemen, excuse me but what are you doing here? We are closed." Paul Kane advanced towards them.

"She's here." One of them pointed out.

"The man she was engaged to disappeared several weeks ago, as a favor to a friend I agreed she could see if this was him."

"So is it him?" The other one asked.

Ema sobbed louder. "Oh sir, I am afraid to look. Mr. Kane has told me this is not a sight for a lady, but I must know."

The first man turned back to Paul, "So what do you think happened to him?"

"Who are you? I cannot talk to you about a body in our establishment, even if his identity is unknown. For the love of God, even suicides deserve some respect."

Both men gazed at Paul.

"Are you newspapermen?" the undertaker asked in an outraged tone. "You must leave right away."

One of them pushed Paul back with his arm, and the other stepped over to the body, and pulled back the sheet. It still lay on its face; the grotesqueness of the spine was apparent. The one holding the sheet looked over his shoulder at his companion. He understood what their next step should be.

"I bet you never saw something like this before, huh?" One of them asked Paul.

"I have seen many bodies with deformities, perhaps that is why this poor soul took his life."

The older one standing next to Ema, took out a revolver, and he pointed it at Paul. "Get the body out of here, I'll take care of them."

"Start the fire in here." The other one instructed and wrapped the blanket around the body like a winding sheet.

Paul's face blanched when he realized these men meant to murder Ema and him. "What is this about?" he stuttered.

The one next to Ema, grabbed her by the waist and nuzzled her neck, "What man would be crazy enough to leave you behind?"

"Please sir, let me leave. You will come to no good end if you persist in this conduct." Ema's tone was like molasses.

The other one with the mummy thrown over his shoulder growled at him, "Kill the bitch."

Ema felt the muzzle of the six-shooter pointed into her midsection. "I warned you Baldy." She said in the same sugary tones, then in the flicker of an eye, she grabbed his hand, pulled it up and pushed the muzzle under his chin pulling the trigger while pushing his body away. Blood and brains splattered across the wall, and his body flopped on the ground.

The man holding the body stared incomprehensibly at his companion who lay on the floor.

He fumbled for his six-shooter still in its holster.

"You sure you want to do that Curtis?" Ema asked in a peculiar, bell-like tone that echoed in the room.

He stumbled backwards. "How do you know my name?" His eyes were round in alarm. Then he shouted, "You're her, shit you're her!"

He threw the dead man's body on top of his companion's bloody corpse and ran towards the door.

Ema started after him.

"Wait!" Paul called out.

"Stoke up your furnace." She shouted out to him as she ran out of the room.

The man she pursued bounced against the walls in his haste to reach the end of the hallway. Ema hitched up her skirts, mentally berating herself for not wearing her trousers. He was no use to her dead.

The man burst through the front door and ran noisily down the boardwalk, his boots clomping on the wood. He glanced back only once, and when he saw Ema pursuing him with her skirts bunched up in her fists, he ran across the road and down an alley.

As Ema ran she transformed; instead of a well-coiffed woman in a costly gown, she took on the appearance of a used up tavern dancer who had seen better days many years before.

The man headed towards a street lined with low-end grog houses which reeked of garbage and refuse. He turned a corner and then stormed through the batwing doors of a saloon with several sailors standing outside. One man who was busy rolling a cigarette, yelled after him for making him drop everything.

A badly tuned piano accompanied a blonde woman with saucy eyes and a low-cut gown that stood on a small stage and sang a ribald song. Raucous laughter, the smell of unwashed bodies and cheap perfume swirled like a heated cloud over the crowd inside.

Ema recognized it as Black Nell's place; named thus because of the color of her heart; she did not have a reputation as a sentimental woman. She stopped outside the doors and then ambled in. She saw Curtis talking to the bartender, grabbing him by the shirtfront. He pointed upstairs, and Ema guessed this was where Black Nell could be found. The man pushed his way through the crowd, scanning the faces looking for his pursuer. He did not register recognition of the blonde woman with frizzled hair and a pockmarked face that followed his movements.

A sailor stepped up to Ema, "Never seen you before, you're not one of Nell's girls. Let's go into the alley and we can settle the deal between you and me." The man grabbed her arm and leered into her face. She leaned in and spoke into his ear.

In a gravelly voice that registered deep in the fear center of his brain, she whispered, "I think you need to leave now." He looked into her eyes that glimmered with a green light. He dropped her arm as if it burned his fingers, and he stepped away from her. It stirred in him a memory of a twenty-footer shark that trailed after their ship for several days when they sailed off the coast of Mexico. It inspired a primal fear in him that perhaps it was waiting for a human body, dead or alive, to fall into the ocean.

Ema followed her quarry up the stairs, threading his way through men that were mounting the steps with a girl, or leaving with a contented smile on their lips. He would look back over his shoulder, but he didn't see the red-haired woman wearing an indigo and lavender dress that shot his partner only a few minutes before.

He clomped to a door at the end of a long corridor. Without a knock he entered. A woman with black hair knotted severely at the nape looked up from a set of ledgers she was writing in. She was flat-chested with a hook nose above thin lips always set in a downward curve. Her calico dress was long-sleeved and plain.

Ema thought none would guess she partnered with several saloonkeepers and ran low-end brothels from their premises. She was as unmerciful as she was rich, and she was quite wealthy.

"Swain, what are you doing here?" she asked in an irritated voice.

"Nell, get me out of the city."

71

The woman stood up from the table. "Why? What have you done now? I told you to stop visiting those faro tables."

"It's not that… "

She interrupted him, "Ducky, if you've got somebody wantin' your hide because you can't pay up, that's your problem, now git outta here."

"She's after me."

"Now you're runnin' from a woman? What hookshop girly did you beat up this time?"

"He's running from me." Ema said from behind the man.

Curtis Swain yelled and stumbled backwards against the table and then sidled over into a corner of the room.

"You fought in the war?" Nell asked disdainfully of the man wedged as far as he could from the woman who stood just inside the room.

She came from around the table and stood in front of Ema. All she saw was a woman wearing the latest fashion, and even her disheveled hair was shiny and caught the light from the lantern. This was the type of woman she hated all her life, blessed with looks fate had cheated her of, but a part of her brain calculated how much money she would make if she prostituted her out to the powerful men on Nob Hill.

"Well, if that don't beat all. What you want im' fer? Did he promise he'd jump the broom with ya' and now he's got cold feet?"

"No, I just want to chat with him a moment, but now that I'm here, I'd like to include you in the conversation. Well not you, exactly."

Before the woman could reply, Ema stepped into the room, pointed at the window and the door and they shut by themselves. The noises from below dulled to an indistinct murmur.

Ema's hair undid itself and swirled around her as if she stood in the path of a breeze but there was none. She held her right hand up and then with her index finger wrote an invisible sigil in the air, and a hole appeared in front of her which widened enough to allow a short staff to jump into her outstretched hand, and then it closed with a pop.

"You!" The woman named Nell hissed.

"Yeah, her!" Curtis Swain yelled from the corner.

"So are you going to come out, or do I have to get you?" Ema asked in a nonchalant tone.

Nell drew back her thin bloodless lips from her teeth and her tongue darted out, then the end of it split open and another bloated, pus-filled tongue erupted. It hung out and made circles in the air as if scenting the location. An odor of tooth decay and undigested food drifted out from her mouth.

Ema eyed the figure up and down. Then she asked, "Is this the slow reveal?"

The man in the corner eyed the door and the window and realized his only exit entailed jumping down two stories.

Black talons erupted from Nell's fingernails, and she brought her right hand to her forehead and pierced the skin. She pushed and blood gushed out, dripping down her face like a scarlet veil. She pulled the nail claw down the middle of the face and kept going, tearing her clothing, the skin and what lay underneath, stopping only when she reached the body's navel. The taloned hands gripped the sides of the flesh and tore it asunder, spilling the woman's innards to the ground. Already a pool of blood and gore inched outward from her feet.

A thing with a beakish mouth exited where the face was before and then like a person shrugging out of their coat, it dropped the body that once housed a human woman. The ripped-open chest cavity draped around its feet. Unable to free itself so soon from its avatar's likeness, the body that emerged still bore a resemblance to a mortal woman. Its ears drooped like a goat, and the lower canines erupted in a burst of blackish blood from the lower gums. The neck thickened and the trapezius muscle became swollen. The toenails sprouted as the foot elongated.

Ema heard flesh tearing and bones crunching as it grew until it towered over her. "Sibylline, have you come to offer me redemption?" The thing growled at her, its head brushing the ceiling.

"I never offer redemption, unless you are asking for it?" Ema asked in a deceptively soft voice.

Ruby eyes dancing with an inner, dark brilliance studied the woman that looked up at it. "Never." Its voice grated within the confines of the room.

"Notus, Bringer of Familiars, what use do you have for an avatar of so little consequence? A whoremonger who trades in flesh?"

"The woman is unimportant; already I have shredded her skin to address you face to face."

"Why her?" Ema persisted.

A thorny spine that lay flat against the creature's back raised itself. The man in the corner whimpered where he lay crouched.

"She gave herself willingly, so what does it matter?"

Ema noticed her question remained unanswered. Notus was a powerful demon that brought familiars to necromancers, warlocks and witches and those who practiced the darkest arts. The familiar owes loyalty to this person even unto their own destruction. Once given over they cannot recall or replace it. They made the bloodiest obeisance to Notus hoping to be rewarded with a mighty familiar.

Ema tapped the staff against her hand, and it glowed neon blue as it grew into a whip that danced and crackled where it lay.

"It matters because I do not take kindly towards those that threatened me or mine. That man did, and he came to her for succor." Ema's tone became flat and unemotional. "You understand what an error it would be to aid those who make war against me?" Ema's voice then changed to something that sounded like a glass bell which no human could produce. Items in the room rattled and bounced as everything inside it quivered. Even the shadows in the room appeared to retreat even though there was no additional source of light.

Notus stamped its feet and snapped its beaklike mouth now lined with sharp teeth. Smoke poured from its nostrils.

"Sibyl, what do I care for what your enemies do? You tend to your souls, and I to mine. If you are wise, then this conversation is at an end." The creature snarled.

Ema's eye lighted with the same aqua light of the whip which she snapped with a twitch of her wrist. It crackled and a line of blue followed in its wake as it traveled through the space between them. "Foolish Notus, I will answer your first question. I do not offer redemption, but I can take you to it, whether or not you wish it. Remember it is not only human souls but others I have dominion over."

The fiendish being stepped back, its eyes following the trail of the whip, knowing that in a millisecond it could open a doorway to another dimension where its power was but a grain of sand in a universe of sand. Crossing The Sibyl had been the undoing of many demons whose fate was unknown. It dared not declare battle against her openly.

Unexpectedly it lunged towards the window, breaking the glass and splintering the frame around the opening as it pulled its body through. With an outstretched claw it grabbed the man cowering on the floor and dragged him behind it. Ema heard it climb onto the roof, then the scream of the man as the creature hurled him down to the street below.

People ran up the stairs to investigate the ruckus. She appeared once more like the rail thin saloon girl as she made her way down against the tide of bodies that flooded into the blood splattered room. She heard women scream, and men swear oaths of disgust. Others vomited the contents of their stomach as they saw what it left of Black Nell.

11.   Transformations

Paul Kane threw wood into the furnace. He didn't know what else to do, his thoughts kept racing around the events he witnessed earlier and what Ema told him. These men came to take the body with them. He realized that if he had been alone, they would have murdered him, and none would have suspected the reason for the crime.

He remembered Ema's warning about how dangerous the knowledge she imparted was, but as an undertaker he believed there was little that could frighten him. How wrong he had been. He realized there was a shadowy underworld swirling everywhere around him, and it was too late to retreat into the ignorance he existed in before.

Paul stopped when he heard a noise from the morgue where the two bodies lay. When he followed Ema out, her carriage stood there with only a little dog waiting inside. The driver no doubt ran away after hearing the gunshot. He locked all the doors of the building, and now the soft rustling sound made sweat break out on his brow.

Then the noise sounded again, louder this time. There could be no mistaking that something moved about inside the room. He had no choice but to see what or who gained entry into the building. He grabbed a poker used for the furnace and crept towards the closed door. Something moved inside there, and he wondered if someone had broken in to steal the body like the first two men. What if it was the first one, and he had hurt or killed Ema?

Paul turned the knob on the door and tightened his grip on the piece of metal. He also prepared to dodge out of the path of a bullet. He peered in, and made out the body of the man shot earlier on the floor, but only the blanket once wrapped around the corpse lay under him. His eyes wandered to the end of the room where a figure scuttled back and forth rhythmically. His mind went blank at what he saw.

It was the man who had hung on the end of a rope for weeks and had lain lifeless on a table in this very room. Now a skeleton with yellowed parchment for skin looked at him with orange flames flickering in the empty sockets of its eyes. Behind it a scorpion's tail made of bone flailed about, the stinger dancing above its head. It extended a bony hand, gesturing for him to come closer. The wet gleam of the dead man's blood still shone on it. There was no tongue in its mouth to speak, so it smacked its teeth, no doubt remembering when it had a voice.

Paul Kane closed his eyes for a moment, hoping that he would open them and find it was all a nightmare. When he opened them, he the living skeleton had fallen forward on its hands, the body elongated and bony legs sprouted from its side. He did not stay to witness anymore of the transformation and ran toward the room where he could get out of this accursed place.

The sound of scurrying echoed behind him, and he dared not look to confirm what he knew followed him. He didn't know if the distance to the door lengthened or if the creature raced faster in its pursuit, but he feared what it would do to him if he fell into its clutches.

Paul opened the door to the outside and saw Ema's carriage. The little dog whined and looked at him through the glass of the window. He grabbed the handle and turned it, knowing he could not outrun the many-legged thing that scrabbled after him. He threw himself inside, and the dog vaulted over his body and landed on the boardwalk barking furiously at the scorpion creature which clacked its appendages threateningly.

The stinger whipped around and struck at the animal, but the dog evaded it and kept barking. Paul watched from inside the carriage, but he knew that if he opened the door, he would fall victim to the horror that even now he could not admit existed.

He wondered when the little dog would tire and failed to dance away in time from certain death. The animal stood still, perked up its ears and howled plaintively, and then it stood on its hind legs and lengthened until it became the size of a human. It was a naked woman with pale skin and long blonde hair, but in an instant she grew even taller, sprouting hair from every pore and claws lengthening her fingers. Her face distorted as a snout erupted forward and her ears grew pointy tufts.

The scorpion creature scuttled backwards as it now faced a wolf with mottled white and gray fur. Standing on its hind legs it towered over 8 feet tall. It gave a deep-throated growl.

The hellish being advanced on the wolf. Its multiple bony legs crackled, and the tail whipped above it. When it struck out with the stinger, the animal's agility was swifter than before. It grabbed the bony appendage, broke off the tip and then swung the body against a wall and then the ground shattering it to bits.

Ema watched from the corner. The streets appeared deserted as most of the crowd congregated at Black Nell's. Upon leaving the saloon she saw Curtis Swain's body draped over a water trough with a broken neck, and a look of horror etched on his features.

She walked up to the giant she-wolf who crouched in obeisance to the woman.

Ema stroked the white fur and murmured, "I know who you are now, and I understand why you were sent to me." The animal whined deep in its throat.

"Well you must assume your identity as Gigi if you are to fit in the carriage."

The transformation reversed itself, like a water-color painting under the rain, until only the little spotted dog sat on the ground.

Ema opened the carriage door, and she found Paul Kane pressed into the cushions on the narrow seat. She climbed in next to him, and the little dog jumped into her lap. The white-haired driver came into view and smiled at the pair then scratched the animal behind the ear.

He looked at Paul Kane, and in a soothing tone said, "Mr. Kane do not worry about the mess, I will make sure everything is clean and I will leave no evidence of what transpired here tonight. Now, where can I take you?"

He whispered an address, and they felt as the carriage swayed and then with a lurch it started forward.

"You no longer recognize the world you live in?" Ema asked him.

"I know you warned me, but I feel I should take the next train heading East."

The woman looked at him with sympathetic eyes. "Paul what if I told you this world exists everywhere?"

He looked at her with worried eyes, "Then I don't know what to do. My brain feels like it'll explode from everything I saw."

"Mort mentioned you are engaged and plan to be married early next year, is that so?"

"Yes."

"Then I will give you my best advice and believe me when I tell you this is not the first time I have held this conversation. Stay here, Paul. Mort and I can protect you, but only…" and she stopped to emphasize her next words, "if you keep quiet about what you saw. As long as they think you are ignorant of the darkness that runs like a river in our world you are safe. It has been thus for thousands

80

of years. You seem like an intelligent man to me, and I believe you'll heed my words."

Paul stayed quiet, eyeing the little dog that looked at him with her head cocked to one side.

Ema continued, "If you decide not to work with us any longer, I will still protect you as long as I am in San Francisco."

"Work with you?" he asked in a hesitant voice.

"Providing information as you did before, nothing more."

He looked down at the little dog again, no doubt remembering its metamorphosis a short time before. "Is everything evil?"

"No, not everything, and like life, there are different degrees of goodness and evil."

He pointed at Gigi. "I saw a woman between the dog and the wolf. Who is she?"

"As a mortal, she committed many atrocious crimes. Someone sent her to me to help expiate her sins and release her into heaven. I believe part of it is because she was also victim to a family curse on her bloodline which she had no control over."

"But why a wolf?" he asked.

"She once went by the name of Assiline Girod, descended from an ancient French family. As a loup garou she terrorized the swamps around New Orleans over seventy years ago. She killed many people, including her own child. I made sure she met her end. It is a tragic tale, and perhaps one day I will tell it to you in its entirety."

The carriage stopped in front of a boarding house in a respectable part of town. Ema placed her hand over his, "Sleep on it Paul. Tomorrow, go into work the same as every day. There will be no evidence of what transpired. The rest is up to you."

He nodded and stepped out of the carriage. It pulled away, and for a moment he stood on the steps leading into the three-story boarding house, looking up at the stars knowing he was now a different man, however he acknowledged a thrill of excitement ran through him because a part of his soul yearned for a challenge, and he could think of none greater.

12. Savages at the Gate

The steamship *Connor* docked in San Francisco. By the time Mort saddled Zabuca, Ema's carriage waited alongside the pier. Father Salazar sat with her, and Mort rode next to them as they headed towards the two-story adobe house on the outskirts of the city.

The priest sat silent, pressed against the side of the conveyance as far as he could get from Ema. She studied him, but did not speak. Once they arrived, she turned to him and said, "Father I have prepared accommodations for you. It is a storeroom next to the kitchen; I have made it as comfortable as possible."

"Thank you." He bobbed his head and practically dove out of the carriage once they stopped.

Soledad opened the door and stood waiting. She met Ema's eyes and came to the priest to guide him inside. The room's one window was small and barred and a heavy lock hung on the door. Inside a comfortable bed, a table and chair filled the space. Soledad came and brought him a plate of food, which he wolfed down. As instructed by Ema she sprinkled a fine powder on it that would make him sleep well into the next day.

Later that evening after Mort had rested he dined with Ema. He told her of everything that occurred since he left San Francisco. Then he pulled out the letters that Father Miel gave him at their first meeting. Outside of each missive was a brief note written by Father Miel, stating that he received these letters by a different courier and not from Father Salazar.

Worded the same, both letters differed only in the instructions written at the end of the one given to Mort. They were both addressed to Ema and read:

Red Lady,

When I thought there was no hope for this situation I find myself in, I came to converse with one who told me of you. His name is Alain Beaupre, and he came to visit Belize City from New Orleans.

At the start of the summer, I worked in a logging camp deep in the jungle. I came across the ruins of an ancient city, stripped of its camouflage by a savage storm that came ashore only weeks before. Excited with this discovery, and despite warnings from the native scout who worked with me to leave the place, I took an artifact encased inside a small box made of some unknown mineral. I will admit that initially I dreamed of finding a city of gold as described by the conquistadors.

It was no dream but a nightmare I brought into my life.

Strange whisperings filled my nights and then shadows flitted through my house. Whatever it was spoke to me in a language I did not know but somehow understood. It demanded blood, it raged in its thirst for it. Then I lost hours during the day when I could not remember where I had been or what I had done. It demanded I should bring it to a place where many sacrifices would be offered to appease it, as had once been done hundreds of years before.

Then strange murders took place in the city of men, women and children, and they could not find the culprit. I realized this occurred during those moments I lost myself.

The last person slaughtered was a man named Father Salazar who had just arrived on a ship in Belize City. It was only I who knew his identity because I discovered his naked body floating in the ocean, and there was none who knew his name. I found all his belongings in my home, and I was dressed in his clothing. The times I am myself are becoming shorter and shorter, but I know that during these times it slumbers inside of me and does not pierce my thoughts.

Among Father Salazar's papers was the name of a man named Alain Beaupre who he was to meet. He described him as a mystic, protected by angels. That is how I learned of you after I met with him.

I also sent a message especially for Brother Miel to accompany Father Salazar through British Honduras and Mexico because I know him to be a fearless warrior in defense of all that is Holy, and he will keep this Devil in rein.

Brother Miel received this letter by a different courier, because I do not trust who I will be by the time I reach San Francisco. I believe the man I am now will not exist any longer. If this letter reaches you in the company of one who claims his name is Father Salazar, do not believe him, for it is me Charles Kydd in the grip of a great Evil that sits at your table.

In Mort's letter he added a postscript.

I do not know your name, but as an emissary of the Red Lady, I beg you that if for any reason this letter does not reach her hands, you will take me and this relic and throw us in the deepest part of the ocean and leave speedily and without a backwards glance.

Ema looked at Mort across the table, and commented, "Well this explains his strange behavior, but why San Francisco?"

"Who asked us to escort him into California?"

"It was a message from Brother Miel." Ema replied with a thoughtful look on her face.

Then she described what transpired in those days since he left. "Mort, I believe those men were waiting for you, and who you were escorting. You yourself noticed that others were tracking your progress besides the party from Rancho Las Margaritas. And I do not believe the explanation that Maria Elena Robles wanted the artifact just to win favor from the local clergy."

"Brother Miel knew a great deal about the Robles family."

"Perhaps then we should ask his help in finding out about Maria Elena before she became the wife of Santiago Robles."

"He said his next stop was the Church of San Miguel Arcángel, in Ixmiquilpan."

Mort then asked, "Ema why do you think they killed the Bloodletter and left him in the abandoned house?"

"Because some, not all of those that belong to the Order of Primus Sanguis cannot help but kill and spill blood. They forget about secrecy. They are disobedient to anything but their compulsion, and if it is true he killed the child Maggie Ryan, whoever brought him here found he was more of a liability than he was worth, even though he had already been part of a ritual."

"Why did he reanimate after so many weeks hanging in that house?"

"The blood of the dead man that spilled on him was the catalyst."

Mort looked at the Ema with serious eyes, "What about the relic? This thing, whatever it is, what will you do with it?"

"I cannot just send it to another dimension. It is powerful, and there are certain steps I have to take in preparation. It will fight to remain here."

"And Mr. Kydd?"

"For the time being we will not disclose that we know his true identity, however he is a very dangerous man. He has been under the influence of this being the longest, he is entirely under its dominion, and it will instruct him to take it away from us."

"Then we must imprison him."

Ema's voice held no regret, "This is what we must do."

Hazel came to where they sat, and asked, "May I join you?"

Mort smiled and motioned her to sit next to them. "Ema has told me what occurred to you."

"Yes, she has been kind enough to let me stay here with her."

"I think it is safer for her until we find out why they attacked her. Mort tomorrow I want you to have a small announcement made in the newspaper that Hazel will reopen her eatery, which she has told me she wants to do. The West End Coffee Shop on the corner of Clay and Dupont Streets is coming up for sale. They found the owner dead of strychnine poisoning. A friend, Dr. Foo alerted me to this opportunity."

Hazel said, "I have money put away, but I had not even looked for a place that I could afford the rent on."

Ema turned to her, "Hazel, I want to help you, but I am hoping to draw out whoever attacked you, or rather who paid those men. We will give you financial backing if you need money."

"Even now, I don't understand why they wanted to destroy my business and hurt me."

"Hazel there can only be one reason, because they know what you are."

The dark haired woman sat silent, looking down at her hands on her lap.

Then she murmured, "Does that mean I should leave San Francisco? I have always been very careful in my activities, but how can I fight against an enemy whose identity is unknown."

87

"You can defend yourself by staying here until we discover who is behind this."

Mort stood up, "Ladies let's step out to the veranda so I can enjoy a smoke."

Once on the second-story veranda, Ema and Hazel sat on comfortable chairs, and Mort pulled out a silver cheroot case. He lit one and looked out over the landscape around the house.

"Ema, what is our next step?"

She looked at both of them. "I am certain there is a particular date where a ritual is being planned. The existence of Notus in this dimension announces that a necromancer is being rewarded with a familiar, and this is not a regular event. I fear that there is a serious threat against many people. Usually this invocation involves the sacrifice of many humans."

Mort looked at a curl of smoke rising from the end of the cheroot. "Ema we are all targets. Will Soledad be safe here if we go to the shop tomorrow?"

"I will leave safeguards behind, but I will consider shutting the house down for a time and she can stay in the shop with us."

The trio spoke of plans, and Mort described his encounter with the ghost of Jack Fletcher, and that he would drop off the will with their solicitor so they could find his daughter. The conversation dwindled and soon they all retired to their bedchambers.

In a well-rehearsed merger, Mort fell into a deep slumber in which Ema, stripped of all clothing melted away into him. The Sibyl and her avatar were one.

The hours slipped away, and the house was silent. Only the sound of insects and the trickle of water from the fountain intruded upon the night.

Mort came wide awake, and he lay still. Then he heard the small dog Gigi who slept on a rug next to the bed whine. Then she growled deep in her throat. He stood up and pulled on his pants.

From the foot of the bed, his six-shooter hung holstered, and he pulled it out. On bare feet he walked quietly down the corridor. The dog followed close behind, still whining. She was alerting to something out of the norm.

He reached the foot of the stairs when Hazel came down the last step and stood next to him. He whispered to her, "Just keep an eye on Soledad, and make sure she is safe." She nodded. Mort heard the shifting of heavy objects coming from the room given to Father Salazar which was close to the kitchen on the first floor in the house's rear. Behind the locked door, noises continued, and then he heard what sounded like a human being panting.

He peered out the window that looked out on the stable and the hill beyond. After becoming a pocket for Ema, his senses had sharpened considerably, including his night vision. Next to him the dog growled and looked at the door leading outside. Then Mort saw movement in the shifting shadows.

A half moon hung in a sky filled with cold stars, providing enough silvery light to illuminate what crept out from the cover of one of the smaller buildings. Against the black and whites etched by the pale orb, it walked out on two feet, but this is where any similarity to a human ended. Its features resembled a cat, and the head sat on a snake-like neck. It had no nostrils, ears or fur of any type. Its body was lean, and it walked in a crouch holding its long arms curled in. Mort estimated that once erect it would be as tall as a man. By its movement he could see it was built for speed and cunning.

Suddenly it halted, belly flattened to the sparse vegetation, it raised its head and sniffed the air. Its face turned, meeting Mort's stare between the space that separated them. The man saw the glitter of death in its catlike eyes, and he could swear it grinned at him with murderous intent.

Then in an instant it bounded towards the outer wall of Charles Kydd's room. Mort knew it headed toward the barred window, but seeing the muscles that rippled under its skin he didn't doubt it could the barrier out of the wall. He reached over to a hook where the key hung. Suddenly he heard a horrific scream coming from the other side of the door.

In that moment he knew the personality of Father Salazar had disappeared and only Charles Kydd confronted a creature beyond his worst nightmare. He heard a crash and when he pushed inside, the creature did as he suspected, pulling the window frame, bars and shutters from the wall.

Its long arm swung in a swift scoop-like motion, extending its taloned hand out. It caught the man by the midsection and dragged him through the opening, bending his body double, breaking his back and any bones that resisted being squeezed through the opening.

Mort stumbled over the furniture that Charles Kydd strewed across the compact room, as if he preternaturally knew what came for him that night. Then he heard a shriek of pain as the creature mauled his captive. Mort reached the opening, and saw it was carrying the man away, holding him by the neck with its oversized jaws. Kydd's limbs flopped lifelessly, and blood and gore trailed after it.

Mort sighted down the gun and opened fire. With a swift movement it jerked aside, and the bullet hit the dead body. The beast dropped it and bounded away into the shadows of the outer building. He did not shoot again, estimating that it was not of this world, and a bullet could not kill it. It accomplished what it came to do, which was killing Charles Kydd.

Then Mort saw the body bubble and disintegrate as it went through the stages of putrefaction in only seconds. A rancid odor drifted on the wind, and then only scraps of clothing remained. He guessed its saliva was poisonous or acted like an acid. He locked the door of the room, securing any entry into the rest of the house. Inside his mind Ema reassured him the thing would not return.

The next day, the group gathered outside after Ema had made a decision to move to the shop for the next few days. Mort drove the carriage with Soledad and Hazel inside. Gigi sat between them. Ema held Zabuca's rein and guarded the saddlebag which held the relic.

The stable hand and other workers who came early in the morning were told to go home and she would send messages to them when they should return.

Once the house stood empty, she walked towards it, and Mort made to follow her. She stopped him and said, "Don't come with me, I am invoking guardians that are dangerous, but this is what we need."

He understood she did it for his protection. These were not heavenly creatures, and Ema was fighting fire with fire. They were not from hell either but from an in-between place that he considered the most dangerous. Beings from this dimension could be invoked, rewarded, placated and sometimes dominated but they were very unpredictable.

He remembered the conversation he had with Ema this morning before the household roused. She disengaged from his body and lay naked next to him in the shadowiness of his bedchamber.

"Mort whoever is behind this is aware of my presence in San Francisco, and they are gambling they will triumph. This points to only one thing, they are trying to bring something powerful into this dimension, a being they think can best me. They dare not assault me directly, because according to Universal Law it would give me permission to defend myself using any of my powers and allies that I can summon, so they are attacking those around me."

"Ema, then what is this artifact that Kydd brought with him?"

She looked at him in the oblique darkness that surrounded them. "Then it is something already here, that only seeks release and our time is short."

13.   What Else is There?

Mort stood next to George Morris. They stared at the carnage. There were five bodies on the rough stones underneath the wharf. One man's chest appeared scooped out as if with a gigantic, saw-toothed spoon. Next to it a torso, untouched except for bloody splatters and that the head and extremities were missing. The narrow chest attested it was a young child. Nearby three bodies lay jumbled next to each other.

George stepped over to one who lay on his face. The stiffening body appeared to have no apparent injury until he turned him over. The front of the face was shredded, as was the throat and chest. Something ripped his lungs and heart from a shattered rib cage. It diced two other bodies in equal portions ready for the stew pot.

The sound of the waves lapping against the stones, and the seagulls calling overhead broke the silence. It was obvious the remains were partially devoured.

George turned to Mort, "I've sent word to the primary district, but finding bodies here is not unheard of. There will be no hurry, and the coroner will respond once the sun is well up and he has eaten his breakfast. I went to your shop to notify Ema because I feel there is something unearthly in all of this, and I think she's the only one that understands what is behind it."

"I am glad you did." Mort said impassively. "She told me what happened in those days I was away from San Francisco."

"Paul Kane spoke of you." Officer Morris replied.

"How did you find out about this murder?"

"I was due to finish my rounds, and I usually stop and talk to whoever is here. Many of them have no job, drink too much and

93

they gather and build small fires to keep warm. This is not the first time I found a dead body here. Murder is common, and self destruction also, but never this butchery." His eyes passed over the corpses.

The sounds of the city awakening increased and a slight breeze came off the sea, carrying the low-tide scent of salt and marine life.

Mort turned to George, "Officer Morris, I hope you will see the wisdom in omitting any mention that I came here. A beast, not a man did this. However there is one who holds its leash, and until we know who this person is, secrecy is one of our most powerful weapons."

George Morris commented, "The murder of Black Nell and Curtis Swain has stirred the deepest superstitions among those who live on the streets. Swain's accomplice, Peterson has disappeared, and many believe he is dead. My superiors in the police headquarters believe a man committed these crimes."

"Just as well." Mort replied.

* * *

It was raining again forcing the stench and smoke of San Francisco downward onto the city. Mort was thankful for a dry and warm place to sit. After a week of chasing shadows and rumors, it was a welcome relief to visit Hazel's cafe. The search for the hellish creature which killed the victims under the wharf, or who ruled over it came to nothing.

Kitchen odors, heavy but appetizing filled his nostrils. The scent of spices interwoven with frying bacon and sausage pervaded the eatery. Mostly men sat at the tables, and Hazel hired two waitresses to help with the constant demand for service. This location was larger than her previous one, but her reputation for tasty and inexpensive food drew a steady stream of clientele through the doors; as a precaution though she slept upstairs from the apothecary shop.

Mort ruminated that he'd been looking in all the wrong places, but he felt in his gut the root of everything was here in San Francisco.

Had it found a lair in an abandoned building? Hunting by night, killing only to eat and not for the pleasure of it, and leaving no trace of its victims, or stowing them in a place where they would be unfound. Even his network in the city that passed reports of disappearances or mutilated bodies provided no solid lead.

The flickering lanterns cast dancing shadows against the wall. Without an introduction a man sat at the table with Mort. Tattoos crept up the sides of his neck. He wore a pea coat and a flat cap. His skin was swarthy, his eyes piggish and furtive. A squat wide nose dominated his face.

He wasted no time with introductions and in a gruff voice said, "He won't be alive long judging by his wounds. It might not be what you're looking for, but I've heard you reward those well who bring you information about killings that aren't a result of a robbery or a brawl."

Mort eyed the man for a moment and then spoke, "Then let's not waste time, take me to him."

"It's down on the Coast."

Mort knew he referred to the Barbary Coast, just east of Chinatown. He followed the tattooed man until they came to a street dominated by saloons and brothels. It was a place full of smells, most of them unpleasant with the occasional scent of the sea laced in it. Music and dancing candlelight would spill from doors that swung open to either discharge a drunken customer or receive a group of men, most of them sailors. Doorkeepers waved over to potential customers, promising the best entertainment awaited inside.

They came to a corner shop, a bakery with two floors above it. Dale Stone, a small-time thug, used the apartments upstairs as an unofficial office. He held high-stake card games there. He also owned some saloons, but he made much of his money by being a rent collector for owners of taverns and brothels. These landlords, most times were reputable businessmen that would not be caught dead at the Coast, so they paid him to pick up money. He also extorted the renters for protection. Two men accompanied him on his rounds to make sure they weren't robbed, or to extract money from those who had fallen behind on their payments.

One of them named Bear, lay on the ground of the bakery where they had dragged his broken body. His eyes were unfocused, and Mort suspected he couldn't see anything.

The baker said, "He works with Dale Stone and I think he fell off the roof or the top floor. Two Chinese dock workers found him crawling down the alley in pain. All busted up, so he fell from somewhere close by. I'd closed up and was down the street when they came and got me."

Bear kept mumbling incomprehensible words. Mort kneeled next to him and looked at what appeared to be jagged bite marks on the man's thick shoulders and upper arms. Bloody spittle frothed out of his mouth. "Got to get out! Get out!" The man raised his voice. He tried to make his lower body respond, but there was no movement. "They're dead, Stone is dead! How in God's name did it get in there?! That devil!" He tried to flail extremities that would not respond any longer to his brain. "Get out!"

Then his breath became a dry rattle and his swollen left eye drifted upwards into his skull. His torture-wearied visage became flaccid.

Mort knew that a killer like Bear would not hurl himself to certain injury or death in fear of a man. He looked up and saw the baker trying to melt into the small crowd that gathered around the dead man. He stood up and in two strides caught him by the scruff of the neck. In a voice full of unmistakable menace, Mort said, "Let's not waste time. What do you know about this?"

The man gulped, but it was apparent he held no loyalty except to save his own skin, "He was upstairs with Stone. Card game, he makes sure nobody's packin' iron, and everythin' remains peaceful like." His eyes shifted away, then he looked again at Mort angrily. "And that's all I knows."

Then out in the street, he heard others shouting and pointing up. He let go of the baker and looked upwards where golden flames winked behind the windows of the second and third floors of the building. San Francisco was no stranger to disease and fire, but the efficient brutality of fire made it the more feared.

Occupants of the surrounding buildings poured out into the street, some of them darted back inside to save their goods, afraid the fire would spread. The rain slowed to a quiet drizzle that did nothing to halt the blaze. The crash of the roof collapsing drowned out the babble of voices in different languages. Debris and sparks showered downwards, sizzling on the pavement.

Mort stepped back with the rest of the crowd. Now there was no way to check on the fate of the occupants of the upper floors, but he would bet they were dead before the fire started. Then he realized the man that brought him there had disappeared. In his experience, he would have been asking for payment once Mort stood over the dying Bear. Such was the nature of business when the trade was only information and he'd met his end of the deal.

The tall, blonde man faded towards the back of the crowd, and looked at the scurrying people just to make sure there was no sign of his informant. Then he thought of the only motive that came to mind, which was to lure him away from Hazel's restaurant. He strode away thinking to hurry back, but once he turned the corner he stopped. The shouts of the crowd faded, and he heard the distant clang of the fire bell.

Hazel served an early supper before she closed which she timed to coincide with dusk. Most of her regular clientele which were dock workers, miners and sailors were headed to their homes or off to a tavern to drink. She would stay behind with her employees and clean up for the following day. This was still two hours away. It was time that he caught up to who was being sent to spy on them. Ema stayed at the shop, guarding the artifact stowed deep in the building's cellar. She warned him that as their deadline came closer, they would become more desperate to attain it, and their measures more extreme.

Mort stopped at the livery on Post Street where Zabuca was stabled. He'd decided this day to go on foot, hoping to be less conspicuous. He traded gossip with the owner, and he left when he saw the daylight fading behind the sullen and slate-colored clouds drifting low over the city.

The livery was only a block away from Hazel's restaurant, and he had a clear line of sight to its doors. The ebb and flow of customers remained normal. He stood there and observed the traffic of men with upturned coats and women with parasols. Carriage wheels squished through the mire, and others on horseback meandered their way through the traffic.

Mort turned down an alley, skirting muddy puddles and circled around until he stood across from the doorway of the restaurant. He made sure he stood under the indigo obscurity cast by the buildings on either side of the passageway. Someone turned over the 'closed' sign on the door, and the last customer exited from the restaurant. Not long after that both women who worked for Hazel left together.

Nightfall arrived and Mort saw what he waited for, a subtle motion within the shadows of a shop gutted by fire a few feet away. It was the same man who approached him earlier in the day. He appeared familiar with Hazel's movements and the time she would leave the business.

She stepped outside, locked the door and looked around with wary eyes to make sure no one was close by. Hazel didn't see the man only a few doors down, who hid behind the brick facade, and in turn he failed to see Mort watching him intently. She settled her wide-brimmed, straw hat firmly on her head and strode off. The tattooed man walked behind her, using other pedestrians to camouflage himself and Mort did the same from the other side of the road.

At the corner she hailed a yellow horse-drawn trolley. The horses' hooves echoed as it pulled the coach along the rails laid down the middle of the road. The tattooed man hurried his pace, but before he could step inside, Mort plucked him by the back of his coat. Wanting to avoid problems, the conductor urged the horses on, leaving both men standing on the steep wooden sidewalk. Mort shook his head when Hazel turned with an alarmed look on her face.

"Didn't expect to see me again?" Mort said in a mock amused voice.

The man tried to pull himself out of the tall man's grasp, with no success. Mort punched him in the mouth and dragged the struggling figure further down the street out of the illumination of the corner gaslight. Then with another yank he threw him into an alley and punched him on the side of the head.

"You son-of-a-bitch let me go!" the man spat out, blood streaming from his lips. He put his fists up and Mort grabbed him by the shirtfront and threw him against the brick of the building, then pummeled him in the stomach. The breath rushed out of him with a grunt.

"Who sent you to spy on Hazel?" Mort's voice was low but with an edge of intimidation that left no doubt he would get answers one way or another.

The man spit out a glob of blood, and Mort hit him once more. "If I don't get answers, gulls will be pecking out your eyeballs come the first rays of daylight, and you'll just be another stupid bastard found dead on the beach."

Then the man's eyes widened as he spied movement behind Mort. A black outline stepped out of the gloom. It appeared to be a huge crow which shrank and then became a live animal which perched on the tall man's shoulder. This more than anything frightened him to the depth of his soul, which was not a simple thing, but his instincts told him he did not deal with things of this world any longer. He committed many crimes against men and women, but he only feared apprehension by the authorities. However in this instant he deemed he was in the presence of something that went far beyond just violence against another person.

"Just to follow her." He spoke in an inaudible voice. "If she went to the apothecary shop or visited another place."

"What else?"

"That's all, and I that I should keep an eye out for ya, that you'd be guarding her. I heard you were lookin' for news on strange happenins' so I used that to make you leave."

"I'm gettin' tired of spoon-feedin' every question to you?" Mort growled.

The man licked his lips. "There's a man Stone delivers the rent money to. He's a gent and works in one of those houses on Nob Hill. He goes by the name of Pill. I never worked for him before. Told me Stone said I'd be good for the job."

The man's eyes flickered in apprehension at the large crow that gazed at him without making a sound.

100

"When were you supposed to report on what you found?"

"Didn't say. Told me he'd find me."

"What's your name?"

"Ivan."

Mort leaned in close to whisper to the man, "Ivan, I've some advice for you. Get out of San Francisco. You saw what happened to Bear, and I'll bet Stone and whoever was upstairs with him, is part of an ash heap. Don't let Pill find you, 'cause it'll be the end of you, whether or not you have information for him."

The man gulped, his strong-boned face which rarely showed fear, quivered with unease, for being an expert in deceit he knew when someone spoke the truth. What he heard was undeniably that.

Mort pushed the man away, who stood for a moment looking at him, and then disappeared into the depths of the alley. The crow cawed once and flitted to sit on Mort's wrist. "Wait for me, I'll be there soon." He instructed, and it took flight wending its way towards the apothecary shop.

14. Come Closer

A bell jingled as the door to the apothecary shop opened.

Miguel Angel, already garbed in his smoking jacket, stood in the gathering gloom next to the entrance. He smiled at Mort and pointed upstairs. He locked the door and pulled down a blind covering the glass.

A fire crackled behind an ornate screen at the fireplace, and the scents of herbs, many of them hung and drying filled the room. In a distant corner, a worktable held those that flourished in darkness. A tall, glass-fronted case held other mixtures reduced to smaller particles with a mortar and pestle. Gigi stretched out next to the warmth, and raised her head once when Mort arrived, and then resumed her nap.

There was another garden on the roof of the building where Ema worked with seedlings and plants. However, this was where she mixed many of the sought-after mixtures and medicines that customers came far and wide for. Now she sat at a worktable that dominated the middle of the room. Hazel sat next to her. The crow perched on a small pile of books. It cawed once when it saw Mort enter, then ruffled its feathers before settling down. As if waiting for his arrival, Soledad came and filled a cup with coffee when Mort sat down. She signaled to Ema, showing that soon she would serve dinner.

"Where shall we start?" Ema asked the small group.

Mort told them everything that transpired that evening. He finished his story, with a question, "The only thing I don't understand is why Hazel is of such interest to whoever is behind this."

Hazel looked at Ema and Mort with a puzzled look on her face. "I don't know. I am nothing special."

Ema interrupted her, "But you are special Hazel, but in ways that are not apparent. Now let us put forth another ingredient into this cauldron of mystery."

Her red hair glinted with the light from the lantern sitting on the table, and her green eyes slid from the face of each of her companions, to a letter she opened. "Paul Kane sent this over today."

She read it to them, "*Remains found. While workmen were engaged in excavating the lot opposite the Presentation Convent on Powell Street, they found a box that contained human bones. The coroner sent the box to me. The land is being prepared for the new Metropolitan Bank, and the coroner has no interest in stirring up gossip so he barely examined what was inside of it. The skeleton belongs to a female child that had been decapitated. The Sisters of the Presentation conducted a school for girls from the convent, including Negro and Indian students. Last year they moved to Taylor and Ellis Streets, however in those last years there was a string of strange disappearance of some of their students, which received little or no notice. I estimate these bones date from the time the girls were students there. I am not sure but I believe this lot belongs to Lane Robinson and has been so for the last few years. It is a name we are both acquainted with. They will bury the child in a pauper's grave for there is no way to tell who she is. Your servant, PK.*"

The flame in the kerosene lantern leaped high inside its glass case, catching the daffodil color of Ema's embroidered gown.

"Before we discuss what this means, Mort we shall learn what is the message that came for you," and she pointed at the crow.

Mort tapped the table in front of him, and the bird obediently jumped down and walked to him. Around one of its legs was a paper secured with a leather thong. He unfurled it and read, "*MER stepdaughter of John Dunbar. Accompanied Stephens and Catherwood as mapmaker to expeditions into the Yucatan to discover ancient cities. Coincidence?*" He turned the paper around and showed Ema a bee drawn in minute detail at the end of the writing.

Their eyes met as they understood this missive originated with Brother Miel. It was obvious he suspected Ema's movements were being closely observed, and instead of sending the dispatch via carrier pigeon, instead chose a messenger loyal to Mort. Only a member of the Sempiterno Apostasy knew of this method.

"Maria Elena Robles' interest is not so mundane after all." Mort commented.

Ema's gaze again swept to each of her companions, "The culmination for this is imminent, but the preparations have been ongoing for years, right under our noses Mort."

He nodded, his eyes troubled.

She continued, "But why now all this recklessness where they have set loose a creature that preys on humans? How much effort have you spent on trying to find it? Men that watch the shop and the house, with no effort to hide themselves."

"Why indeed?"

"I recently gave a friend advice that I have failed to act upon myself."

Mort looked intently at her because he knew the answer before she said it.

"Distractions, only distractions. To buy themselves what they are desperate for, time."

"But certain events have forced their hand." Mort added.

"Yes, Brother Miel sending for you to escort the imposter Charles Kydd through California, the discovery of the Bloodletter's corpse in the abandoned house and the sacrificial site Hazel found in the forest."

"These two messages we have received Ema... "

Hazel interrupted Mort, "I am sorry, but I must speak," the dark-haired woman turned to Ema, her dark eyes shiny, "I cannot wait another night without shifting."

Ema studied her face, already the area above her lips appeared swollen, and the cheekbones and brow bones were more pronounced.

Hazel continued, "I have heeded your warning to stay close, but this is beyond my control, and for this delay I cannot just become a regular cat, I must transform to something larger."

"Then I will go with you. Can you wait a few minutes?"

"Yes," her smile was grateful.

"Then go to the roof, and I will be there soon."

Mort followed Ema upstairs to their apartment. She stripped off her gown, and undergarments. She spoke to him in the meantime, "Mort you must stay and guard the way into the cellar, but you must not open the door under any circumstances. Even if you hear a noise down there, or my voice calling out to you, ignore it. Do not be drawn outside the house. The heart of this thing is a serpent named deceit, a fact that its followers have realized too late in their existence."

Mort nodded. Ema stood before him naked, her full breasts and the regal lines of her body as familiar as his own. Lamplight cast shadows on the curves of her figure. She signed a sigil in the air and a slight distortion shimmered in the space, and then it puckered, allowing several moths to flutter around her. Two comet moths perched on each shoulder, their colors of gold and purple melted and became a tight-fitting armor around her entire body.

The pigments swirled around in slow motion as she moved. Her coiffed hair undid itself into a single long braid where a brightly colored elephant hawk-moth attached itself to the end as an exotic ornament.

The scent of night blooming jasmine filled the room.

Then Ema whispered, "Zeruko Neskamea." She pushed her hand into the space and drew out her sword made of Toledo steel, with a pink diamond gracing its pommel surrounded in silver. Strange symbols were carved on it. Then an etched dagger, out of the space where it patiently awaited its mistress, jumped into her other hand. "Iron Horse," she murmured and smiled. They created these instruments during the times of ancient civilizations. Then the suit on her back, split in a long groove where she placed the sword and the dagger she slipped into her abdomen, with only the pommel protruding out.

"By dawn?" Mort asked.

She only nodded her head.

* * *

Once on the roof, Ema found a pile of Hazel's clothing. Out of the gloom an enormous cat padded forward, and she recognized it as a black jaguar with hidden rosettes marking its fur.

Then she opened her right hand palm upwards and a small, blue cubicle appeared there, gyrating slowly. She tossed it in the air, and it swirled in mid-space, elongating until a tall physique took shape. A muscular man's figure with a jackal's head towered over her. His skin was blue, and he held a thick spear. It bowed to Ema, who in turn greeted him in similar fashion. In a language unheard of in thousands of years she said, "Guard my home."

It strode to the wall and melted into the brick.

"Take me to the altar." She said to Hazel, who watched with incurious eyes.

The animal leaped to an adjoining roof, and Ema followed with ease. She made her way towards the edge of the city, and then off into the sand hills. Before long they came to the place Hazel described. Nothing moved but a few lingering drops of rain borne along by the wind. Listening, she heard no other sound, and the smell of wet, charred wood lingered. In the main altar rainwater gathered in the hollow, tinged with blood and strands of gore. The four bodies were gone, however Death visited but only a short time ago.

Hazel paced along the perimeter but did not enter. Inhuman creatures that attended the sacrifices hissed and opened a passage for the red-haired woman. They feared this one greatly, she was not merciless by nature, but by choice. She was the key to the place where they could not survive as they were, the Place of Endless Light, where none cast a shadow. This existence was anathema to them. But something trapped them within this circle, bound to serve and could not escape her.

"Bring me the spirit of the one killed here today." Ema commanded.

The creatures tittered and resisted. One slithered on the ground in a boneless motion until it pulled itself erect. Reptilian eyes blinked from its face. A head ringed in bristles and quills crowned it, and a pale, pasty tongue hung from the edge of its frog-like mouth. The rancid odor of decaying flesh hung like an invisible pall within the circle.

It communicated in noises not known in this dimension, which passed as its language, "No, we are here at the behest of another who feeds us blood as agreed in our covenant. We have done nothing against you. You are powerless to exact obedience from us."

107

Ema responded in measured tones, "I have done nothing against you either; all I asked for is the spirit of the one whose blood is still wet on the altar." The armor encasing her skin, darkened to a deep violet color.

"No." The creature said with a note of finality.

"Was this a willing sacrifice, that you claim it so fiercely?"

"No." The demon repeated.

Ema smiled, but there was no mirth in it. She said scornfully, "You are correct, I have no dominion over you now, but I have authority over that human spirit. You should have agreed to bring it to me, for now I will fetch it."

A powerful wind picked up around the trees, and a howling filled the space. Evil spirits, more ancient and wiser than the one who spoke to Ema, cried out in dismay.

"We will bring her Great Sibyl, ignore this foolish one." Many of them grunted in protest.

Ema shook her head, "I have fulfilled my obligation by offering you a chance to accommodate my request." In a swift motion, she pulled out her sword and jumped on the piece of timber that measured six feet across. She plunged it into the center. Immediately a shaft of white light shot up into the sky, and the screams of those who guarded it cried out in anguish and fury. A wave of pearlescent vapor dripped off the edges and crept on all sides of the circle, covering the ground trickling towards the edges.

The clamor increased, reaching a crescendo and the flow of incandescence reversed itself as a whirlpool whipped around her ankles sucking everything into it. Ema jumped off, watching creatures of unimaginable horror, unseen ever by human eyes, never to be part of this world swirl towards the center of the vortex.

Then she saw the image of a human face among the multitude. Her mouth opened in a silent scream of terror. Ema pushed her hand into the cyclone of creatures and pulled the woman out. The suction increased, and it sounded like a locomotive bearing down upon them. In an instant the light vanished, and a total silence blanketed everything, every screech ceased.

The petrified tree trunk crumbled inward. Then the sounds of the forest swept in as nature claimed its domain once again. The desecration made against the land was erased, and insects and night animals came close without fear.

Hazel who'd paced from the boundaries of the circle, now sauntered towards Ema, and swept across her legs, laying down close by. "Go hunt something and come back quickly." She said to the jaguar which growled once and ambled into the underbrush.

Then she turned to the figure of a woman who stood before her. Her death was recent, and she appeared in full color as she did when she met her fate. She tried to talk, but the neck had been almost severed off her shoulders, and her vocal cords did not work.

"Speak to me with your mind, you are dead and can no longer talk." Ema said straightforwardly to her. Like a far off echo, the woman's voice filled Ema's thoughts. The hysteria and frenzy of her speech made her words incomprehensible.

"Slow down," she urged the woman, whose mouth still opened and closed like a dying fish, "tell me your name."

"Mildred, Mildred Pill."

Ema saw where the woman's high-collared shirt and corset were ripped open. A gaping hole in her chest with jagged skin flapping along the edges confirmed they had extracted her heart with a crude instrument. Blood streamed down to the end of her skirt which swept the ground. Ema saw fingerprints where they had bruised her wrists while holding her down. Her ebony hair clung to her face and forehead.

"Who did this to you?" Ema asked.

"I don't know!" The woman screamed in her head.

"Describe what happened."

"We drank our afternoon tea, and then I felt tired and could barely keep my eyes open. We lay down for a few minutes, and then I awoke here, in this place surrounded by four figures cloaked in black. I could not see their faces. They would not speak to me, and then they held me down, and one of them spoke in a language I couldn't understand."

The woman's eyes became wild as she remembered the moment of her death.

"The moment has passed and they cannot hurt you any longer." Ema reminded the woman. "You recognized no one in the group?"

"No, only that they were all men."

"Are you married, do you have a family?"

"Yes, my husband and my daughter."

"Where are they?" Ema asked gently.

"I am the housekeeper for Lane Robinson, and my husband Gideon Pill is Mr. Robinson's valet. He and my daughter Lynne, they must be so worried for me."

Ema observed that even dead, this woman fretted for her family.

"Where are they now?"

"At the Occidental, Mr. Robinson sold his home, and will stay at the hotel until his new mansion is complete. They are breaking ground on it tomorrow. It will be so beautiful, there on Nob Hill. I stayed behind at the other house to make sure everything was tidy. Lynne and I would close up the house tomorrow. I must tell them where I am."

Ema looked at her with compassion; she knew this part would be difficult as it was for humans who died in these circumstances. "Mildred, you are no longer alive. They committed a great crime against you, and they brought you to this place to murder you."

It was then that the specter looked down at her clothing and saw the shredded shirt and the gaping hollow in her chest. Her eyes traced the scarlet river made by her life's blood that stained her garment. She fingered the pocket watch chained to the lapel of a short jacket she wore as if in remembrance when telling time had importance.

Ema knew this undeniable proof of her death would be the easiest way to release her on her way to the afterlife. She watched Mildred's face twist with uncommon emotions. Then she asked, "My daughter, what will become of her? Will they hurt her? Why did they kill me?"

"If I look after your daughter, will you accompany him?"

"Who?" The ghost asked with questioning eyes.

Ema stepped aside. An older man with silver, shoulder length hair, wearing a long duster and stove-pipe hat smiled at Mildred from the edge of the woods. He walked towards her. "My name is Miguel Angel, I heard that you are lost and need an escort."

"Yes," she answered uncertainly. "Miguel, isn't that Spanish for Michael?"

"So it is Mildred. May I call you Mildred?"

She nodded, and he proffered the crook of his arm to her. She placed her hand there, and he led her away. His voice was gentle, "I will protect you now." She looked back once at Ema and turned trusting eyes to her companion. They dissolved as they entered the woods, pearls of light flitting around them and disappearing into the branches above.

From across the circle, a whisper drifted towards Ema, "Sibylline, I am here in answer to your summons."

Ema turned to the tall, thin figure that emerged and entered the circle. A cloak of green leaves draped the figure that held a staff intertwined with vines. The hands were human like but only had four fingers. A cowl covered most of the face except the cherry-tinged lips. The skin was the color of a peridot, and the smell of fecund, damp earth followed in its wake.

"Thank you," Ema continued, "I have burned away the stain on this piece of land, but I dare not leave it unattended where it could be used once again in rituals that strip away its power of creation."

"But all you need is to lay your hand upon the soil, and life will spring forth." The figure said.

"Fresh life is defenseless; we must establish the cycle of birth, death and rebirth and there is no fiercer guardian than you. Erase all remnants of the sacrilege committed here. That is all I ask."

"And so it shall be, Walker Between the Worlds."

A whirlwind danced into the circle, and the leaves of its cloak fluttered free in disarray, and the staff softened and the vines fell to the ground, digging themselves into the soil. The protector disappeared.

Ema kneeled and kissed the shriveled tree trunk. Mushrooms erupted, with evening primroses among them. The earth disgorged angel's trumpets, devil's trumpets and night phlox which inched towards the edges of the barren circle. Some twined themselves around Ema's legs and crept up into her braid.

She stepped outside the circle. Hazel came out of the shadows to meet her. The jaguar sat on her haunches and looked up at the woman.

"We're going to Nob Hill," Ema said.

15. Primus Sanguis

Sand dunes covered in scrub, tidal inlets and swamps edged Mission Bay in the distance. A three-quarter moon bounced off the seawater casting a metallic tint to the expanse seen from the empty mansion on Nob Hill. It was ornate, with turrets and spires, but still under construction. The area was lonely as most of the well-to-do lived on Rincon Hill. Now they were erecting even more ostentatious mansions on this elevated piece of land that overlooked the city.

Ema and Hazel waited on the roof, next to one of several jutting chimneys decorated with intricate corbels. From this vantage point they could see a property downhill from them. Construction had yet to begin, and they had leveled only the ground, ready for the partitioning of the cellar that would make up the mansion's foundation.

A ramshackle shed with tools scattered about stood in the corner. Two men sat outside it, a lantern hung on a hook casting a golden orb of illumination. The clop of horses' hooves sounded out. A carriage climbed slowly up the steep incline.

Ema whispered to the jaguar who sat patiently next to her, "Wait here, and keep an eye out for late arrivals." The animal licked its chops in answer. She made her way stealthily down, and hid behind the shed, watching as two men alighted from the carriage.

A tall one, with bulbous eyes and a roadmap of veins on his nose went to where both men sat. They stood up and bobbed their heads. There was no disguising the fear they felt for this man.

"You two, get on outta here." He pointed to where the carriage waited with his thumb. "If anyone asks you weren't here, and neither was I. You know I'm no scaley feller and give rewards

113

where they're due. So if I hear either of you jawin' to anyone, by God I'll take a scraper to your throats, and that's the last talkin' you'll be doin' this side of hell."

"Yes, Mr. Pill." Both said unison.

Once both men were seated inside the carriage, Pill's companion instructed the driver to take them down to a saloon on the Barbary Coast named Sweet Tilly.

"Gentlemen, just tell Tilly Mr. Pill sent you. I have instructed her to give you special treatment."

The men smiled at each other in anticipation, however one said to the other as they settled in their seat, "That Pill, he's savage as a meat axe."

Unknown to them, Tilly's instructions were to drug and shanghai them. She knew of a British ship anchored in the Bay, soon to leave for Australia, which was short of men to do menial jobs. She would split the money with Pill. It was only the profit from selling them that decided their fate should be slavery on a boat instead of a knife in their ribs.

Once the carriage pulled away the second man, shorter with a long beard waddled to where Pill waited for him. His protruding belly strained the buttons of his vest. He said, "It's close to midnight."

"Perfect," Gideon Pill replied, "once we are at the thirteenth hour, then we bury the offering."

He opened the door to the shed and dragged out a stumbling teenage girl that wore a thin muslin nightgown. Her strawberry blonde hair hung to her waist, and she shivered in the chilly night air. She blinked in the light coming from the lantern.

"Should we drug her more?" the squat man asked.

"Nah, she needs to die slow, but bring some extra rope and a shovel."

Tears slid from the girl's eyes. Her voice shook, "Mr. Pill, where's my ma? Why did you bring me here and treat me like this? I know you've no love for me, but you're married to my mother."

Pill grabbed her by the hair and pulled her along towards the planned entryway of the house. "Your ma is dead. I killed her." His voice was cold and unemotional.

The girl cried out in heartbreak, and he threw her to the ground. Then the other man came to stand beside them. He held the lantern in one hand, and the rope and shovel in the other.

"So Pill, seems a shame to let such a pretty thing like this go untasted." His eyes ran up and down her slim body with lascivious intent blatant on his face.

"Gallotti you dolt, a virgin she must stay."

The girl continued to cry, oblivious to their conversation.

"So Pill, how you gonna explain the disappearance of the Missus and her daughter?"

"I already hinted they might return to Missouri for a spell while the house was being built. My wife has people there. I'll just say she left me and went off to New York instead of returning."

Ema watched from the shadows, listening to their conversation. She knew already what their plans were, but let them continue hoping they would disclose more.

What they intended was a custom dating back to the most ancient of civilizations. Imprisoning the live person in the foundation to assure the building, bridge or other structure would be durable, as well as becoming its guardian. Some rituals demanded a pure, sexually innocent victim who suffered the slow death of being buried alive.

Pill leaned down and pulled away a canvas that covered where steps would lead to the main doorway of the house. A rectangular, deep pit stared back at them. In that moment, it dawned on the girl what their intentions were. She tried to stand up and run away. Pill grabbed by her long hair, clapping a hand over her mouth.

Gallotti set the lantern down, dropped the shovel, and walked towards the pair with a length of rope.

"I'll put her in the pit, and you can drop the dirt on her when the time is right. I still don't get why I can't spend some time with this dainty little morsel, who's going to… "

The pommel of Iron Horse protruding from under his chin eclipsed the rest of his words. Between his blood-stained lips, the glint of the blade winked, and his eyes arched backward into his skull as if in search of the point that pierced his brain.

Gideon Pill stood for a moment immobile, and then he threw the girl to the ground with a rough shove. He reached for a knife on his belt, and Ema kicked him viciously on the kneecap. The sound of cracking accompanied his howl of anguish. He bent to grab his knee, and in a flash she pulled the dagger out of Gallotti's head, and used its pommel like a hammer to strike Pill on his kidney. He screamed and went down on his other knee, and Ema pulled the weapon from his belt.

Pill stared up at her, hatred shining in his bulbous eyes. Her gaze slid down to his hand, where between his thumb and forefinger a tattoo of the Primus Sanguis proclaimed his allegiance.

Her voice hardened ruthlessly, "So who holds your leash, Pill? A Bloodletter always has a master."

He could not hide his startled expression; few knew about the Order of Primus Sanguis.

In a contemptuous tone he answered, "I'll not answer ya, bitch! I ain't no rat. If not her, it'll be another. If not this house, we'll find someplace else."

"Is it Lane Robinson?"

He attempted to stand up on his one good leg, "Ears plugged?" He asked derisively. "I ain't afeared of ya. Go ahead use that piece of cold steel on me and get it over with."

Ema studied him, learning more from his lack of words than what he said. Little did he know how well she knew the characteristics of those who claimed membership among the Primus Sanguis. His path to purgatory would lie through her, because otherwise he was destined to escape the law of men.

"Are you sure you've nothing to tell me? As much as I detest you, I'd much prefer to take the one ordering all these rituals."

His eyes raked her form, never had he seen a woman dressed this way. He'd seen plenty of saloon girls and whores with just a skimpy dress on or nothing at all. Till this moment he thought she was just a myth, a story told among those who existed in the obscure but ever present world of necromancy that flowed in every city he visited. The advice had always been the same from those who held knowledge of her, which was to avoid the Sibyl at all costs. However she seemed so ordinarily human; beautiful with a bad temper, but just a woman.

She lowered her voice, almost wheedling she asked, "Third time's a charm, there's no name you want to volunteer?"

Then out of the underbrush Hazel padded forward. The sight of the jaguar erased the man's defiant smile. It growled at him, and the fear in his eyes was genuine and stark.

The girl who lay on the ground, covering her face, stood up and stepped behind Ema for protection.

"Lynne listen me." Ema said in a soft voice to her.

The girl looked at her with wide eyes, then Ema touched her finger to a spot between her eyebrows, and her eyelids drooped and the tension left her body. "Go with the jaguar, she will not harm you. There is no fear."

The girl stumbled towards Hazel, and Ema said, "Take her away from here, stay close by, but neither of you should witness what will unfold."

The enormous cat walked towards Lynne, grabbed her hand gently between her pointed teeth and pulled her along a bit. She let go. The girl followed the jaguar through the trees and they disappeared.

Somewhere far off a clock struck twelve. "What good timing." Ema murmured.

Using Iron Horse as a pointer she outlined a circle in the space before her. Into her hand jumped a short staff that instantly elongated and became a whip which crackled with a blue light. Then with a forefinger she touched the edge of the circle, and like a lasso she lengthened it and threw it around where she stood with Pill.

Despite his false bravado, Pill gulped, and said, "So get it over with."

"What did they promise you, that you'd be immortal? That they'll bring you back from the land of the dead to command black spirits on their behalf?"

The man looked at her without saying a word. He tried to straighten out his coat and the vest underneath, then his hand went to his tie as if it was too tight.

"Never mind, you've answered my question." Ema said in a mocking tone.

Then Pill's head whipped around as if he heard a sound he couldn't quite make sense of. A fog crept in, not from the bay but from the edges of the circle and it slithered along the ground towards the center. It covered Ema and Pill's legs up to their knees. Growls and moans increased in volume, and murky figures solidified. They rose out from the fog.

"What is this?" Pill asked in a quavering voice.

"A reunion." Ema answered.

Then a howl sounded out, which lowered and ended with a word, "Gideon." A thing on two legs stepped forward accompanied by the sound of large hooves.

Pill's eyes raised to the thing's face and the emaciated features he recognized at once. It belonged to a man he knew only as Durand, a Bloodletter who deserted the Union army during the Civil War when his sadistic actions came to the attention of his superiors. He joined any gang of guerrillas or desperados roaming the countryside that did not interfere with his propensity for torture. They'd crossed paths once when he'd set up a small office as a doctor outside St. Louis, but here he was now in front of him. An emaciated figure with protruding ribs, and an elongated neck advanced towards him, and the only part of it as human was the countenance. Antlers towered above it with shreds of skin and bloody gore hanging from it.

Then Pill looked around him and saw he was ringed with figures, some similar, but different. More horrific than anything even someone with his putrid mind could come up with. Some of them were Bloodletters he met throughout his travels.

The beasts slavered, and those who knew him called out, "Brother come we have something to show you. Practices beyond anything you could imagine."

"No!" Pill screamed and tried to back away.

Ema stepped out of the circle, the figures giving her a wide berth and casting their gazes downward.

The Durand creature stepped forward, holding a sharp meat hook in its elongated fingers. Pill recognized it as something he learned to use in the slaughterhouses of New York and Chicago. It was in these places he mastered the art of butchering a human or an animal.

119

Ema's voice faded to a hushed stillness, "They lied to you. I don't. You're on the path to purgatory, a reward you don't deserve now, but once did, before it corrupted you."

Incomprehension etched itself across Pill's face, and he made to follow her. The meat hook flashed overhead, and it caught him under the chin, the tall creature jerking him off his feet where he dangled. The others in the group surged forward and crowded around him. Some of them licked, others gnawed with crooked teeth on his flesh.

Ema's whip whistled in the air, and the scene folded into a large teardrop shape, which poured itself into a slit with darkness on the other side. Again she snapped the whip, and the tear mended itself.

On the other side of the bushes Lynne laid curled up on her side, her head resting on the jaguar's belly. The beast's fur kept her warm. Ema heard the flapping of wings and looked up. A large crow stared down at her from the branches.

She stooped down and hoisted the girl over her shoulder. Then to the crow she said, "Tell Mort I'll be home soon, and we've got a new houseguest."

* * *

Ema pulled the blanket over Lynne's shoulder, and the girl's breathing was even as she slept. She made up a bed for her on a chaise lounge outside the bedroom. Mort watched her, and realized as he had done several times through the years he'd accompanied Ema, the deep well of empathy and tenderness she harbored in her being.

Hazel, now a woman once again, went off to the small bedchamber she used in the back area of the shop on the second floor.

THE PATH TO PURGATORY

Ema walked into the bedroom and Mort closed the door behind them. The covering on her body shrank, and all that was left were two large moths on either shoulder. He opened a small window, and they flew out into the night. In a custom repeated many times, Mort stretched out on the bed, and immediately he fell into an all encompassing lethargy. Ema melted into the body of her pocket.

16.   The Darkest Hour

Ema, Mort and Hazel were already eating breakfast the following day when Lynne came to the table. Soledad found a shawl for her to wear. The girl's face was somber, and she remained quiet and made no move to eat any of the food.

Ema asked her, "Lynne, what do you remember about yesterday?"

The girl looked up at her with eyes full of unshed tears.

Her voice trembled as she spoke, "I spent the day with my mother, making sure the Robinson's old house was tidy. We drank some tea, and I remember my mother said to lie next to her because she would take a quick nap. I felt sleepy too. Then I woke up inside the shed."

The girl took a deep breath, trying to stop herself from crying out loud. "Mr. Pill grabbed me, tied me up and said he killed my mother."

Hazel rubbed her shoulder comfortingly. "Then you arrived," she continued, "and I remember little after that, except when I woke up this morning."

Ema nodded and considered a moment before speaking. "Lynne, I wish I could say that Mr. Pill lied about what he said about your mother, but it is the truth." The teenager cried openly. "If there is any comfort I can give you, is that Mr. Pill is being held responsible for what he did, and you will ever see him again. Do you have any family in San Francisco?"

She shook her head. "My only family lives in St. Louis, my aunt, uncle and cousin live there."

"Would they welcome you if we sent you there?"

Lynne's eyes shone with hope. "Yes they would. My aunt kept asking my mother to send me to her, and momma was ready several times, but Mr. Pill would talk her out of it. But then he acted like he couldn't stand the sight of me."

Ema gazed at the girl and asked, "Lynne, how old are you?"

"Fourteen."

"In a short amount of time they have cruelly stripped you of the slow transition to womanhood, and I need you to listen to what I will tell you." Ema said.

The girl nodded and looked at the face of the other adults there. The blonde man with a mustache smiled at her encouragingly as did the dark-haired woman with the kind eyes who sat next to her.

"I do not think it is safe for you in San Francisco. To protect you, I think we should send you to your family in St. Louis as soon as possible. I will write a brief letter to your aunt, describing how your mother died at the hands of Mr. Pill, but he is dead now. In the meantime we will send a telegram to let them know when you will be arriving."

Lynne said in a quiet voice that still trembled with unshed tears "Aunt Sarah never liked Mr. Pill. She came to visit two years ago, and they did not get along. Momma married him five years ago, because after my father died we were having a hard time getting food to eat and having a place to live, and I think momma's pride wouldn't let her return to St. Louis because she married my father against her family's wishes."

"What about Mr. Robinson, did you meet him?"

The girl shook her head. "Not really, I would see him arriving in his coach or talking to guests in the garden. Him and his wife seem like pleasant people, but there were always lots of businessmen coming to see him. Their two sons are studying back East. I could tell though that Mr. Pill acted differently around Mr. Robinson."

"What do you mean?" Ema asked her.

"Well, he was always courteous, and wouldn't curse or use any of the terrible words he said to my mother or the other servants. He made sure that the only one who did anything for the Robinsons was him."

"Very well, Lynne. I will get some clothing made for you. Soledad will come later to take your measurements. You must stay inside, I have books you can read. Hazel has agreed to accompany you to Missouri."

The girl smiled, and then said, "I would like to see the little dog. I woke up in the night she snuggled up next to me. Can I play with her?"

"Yes her name is Gigi."

Upon hearing her name, the dog bounded out from under the table to sit next to the girl.

Lynne said, "Thank you for sending me to my family; I was afraid I would have to go to the Magdalene Asylum which I've heard is a horrible place."

Then she excused herself and Gigi followed her to the chaise lounge next to the fireplace on the other side of the apartment.

Ema turned to Hazel with a smile, "I know you've just opened the restaurant, but I have plans for someone to cook there in the meantime, and make sure you don't lose the good reputation you have with your customers." Then her face became somber, and she continued, "But the same as Lynne, for the time being your absence in San Francisco is better for you. We still don't know why Pill wanted to have someone follow you around, but knowing what he's been up to, I am positive it is dangerous."

Mort said tersely, "The question is to find out who Pill is working with."

Hazel asked, "Lane Robinson, or do you think there're others?"

Soledad entered with the morning newspaper which she handed to Mort. In her other hand she held an envelope made of creamy

124

paper and engraved with a stylized 'R' in the center. This she laid before Ema.

Mort scanned the newspaper and smiled mirthlessly, "No doubt this has made the front page because of Robinson's name." He read the article,

> *"A Dead Man Found - etc.*
>
> *Between 5 and 6 o'clock this morning, they found the body of a man named Pietro Gallotti on the grounds of Mr. Lane Robinson's new mansion on Nob Hill which was due to start construction this week. He was savagely stabbed through his head, and strangely the wound was cauterized as if the instrument used was burning hot. Several pools of blood were found, so much more than can be accounted for by Mr. Gallotti's body. There is now grave concern for Mr. and Mrs. Gideon Pill and their daughter Lynne which have disappeared. Mr. Pill is Mr. Robinson's personal valet, and Mrs. Pill was the housekeeper. To add to this mystery several paw prints of what some have identified as an enormous cat, possibly a cougar were tracked in proximity to the crime scene. Police are investigating and the coroner has received the body pending an inquest."*

Mort scanned further, smiled and looked at Ema, who smiled back. A knowing look passed between them. He read,

> *"Officer George Morris along with several other policemen made a dawn raid on a notorious saloon, Sweet Tilly located on the Barbary Coast. There have been rumors for some years that men would disappear from the premises, kidnapped to serve against their will on outgoing ships. The police found several men tied up in the cellar, ready to be handed over to the captain of the British ship, Goliath, bound to leave in two days to Australia. They made*

several arrests, including the owner Mrs. Tilly Knight and others who work there. They are to appear before the judge this morning."

With a raised eyebrow, Mort said, "It seems you had a busy night after all."

"Well, they addressed this invitation to both of us, let us see what this is about."

Ema scanned the document and then passed it to Mort. It was a request for both of them to attend a luncheon at the Occidental Hotel the following week. Mr. Lane Robinson wanted to announce the construction of The Metropolitan Bank opening the following spring.

"Coincidence?" Mort asked.

"Perhaps for them, but not for us." Ema said with finality.

* * *

Ema kept Hazel and Lynne close to the shop. She contracted with Dr. Foo to have a Chinese cook take over at the restaurant which he assured her he would oversee the person assigned to the task.

She visited her personal dressmaker with Lynne's measurements and ordered clothing that would be ready within seventy-two hours after her initial visit. She sent a telegram to Lynne's aunt in St. Louis. She did not mention her by name, only referred to the girl as her niece, and that they would send a notice with the exact time and date of her arrival. Ema did not know who Pill had on his information payroll, but someone at the telegraph office would be an obvious pick.

The week sped by and it was the evening before the luncheon, when Ema and Mort left the shop each astride a horse. Ema on Zabuca, and Mort on the gelding used for the carriage named Zeus.

126

THE PATH TO PURGATORY

The gaslights were being lit, and the sunset cast lengthening shadows. They rode towards the future site of the Metropolitan Bank. Once there, they dismounted and stood across the street. Towards the back of the lot were four immense statues of reclining lions each on a pedestal. A newspaper article described where each statue would be erected at the four corners of the building, and that Lane Robinson paid a sizeable sum of money to have them shipped from New York.

Ema saw what she expected, and she sighed wishing she had been mistaken. She turned to Mort, "Do you see them?"

Mort squinted, after becoming Ema's pocket his ability to see the dead expanded to see restless spirits in the most unexpected places, but now he saw a shimmer in front of each statue.

"You might have a minor difficulty because they are purposely being obscured. But keep watching." Ema instructed him in a soft voice.

Then everything came into focus and he saw a naked man standing in front of each statue. They wandered back and forth and around the perimeter of the base of the effigy, but never far from it as if an invisible chain held them in place. Each displayed red, livid scars in certain parts of their body. They all corresponded to the wounds described by Hazel of the four men found butchered in the forest. The ultimate confirmation came when one of them turned, and the tattoo of the full-rigged clipper ship dominated his back as Hazel had described.

"Ema what is this?" Mort asked.

"Something similar to what they were planning to do with Lynne. They anchored each of them to a statue, representing guardians at the four directions. The centerpiece is something much grander, and I think I understand better the interest in the artifact."

Ema spoke in a quiet voice, describing what she witnessed more than once throughout history, "Mort, the demon housed in that relic promises success and triumph. Emperors and their generals would carry it into battle and feed it the blood and death of their enemies. However the day arrives when conquest is complete, and then this demon still demands tribute. There is no peace to be found after they have vanquished the enemy. Then those in power give it prisoners, criminals and those who do not serve society. When they stop, they learn the awful truth of the bargain they have made. The people are visited with famine and pestilence. So then they turn over the most select of their society, such as unblemished children. The priests who guard it lie to the populace and tell them it is an honor to be chosen as a sacrifice. This is a temporary measure, for this thing is never satisfied unless there is wholesale slaughter and suffering."

Mort looked at the pacing spirits of the men, who appeared trapped in the hell imposed on them by the last few moments of their life.

"Is that what happened to the civilization that lived in the ruins where Kydd found it?"

"Yes, they had no other choice but to abandon their city, trap it in a special reliquary and then perform rites to seal it."

"But why here?"

"It is doing what it has always done. Find a human or a group of them whose thirst for triumph at all costs blinds them to the horror of what it asks for in exchange. The place where it was worshipped sits abandoned and hidden by jungle. Look around Mort, this place is full of life and everyday ships, trains and stagecoaches bring additional people to live here."

Mort looked down at her, and his fair eyebrows slanted in a frown. "So who is using it now, Lane Robinson with his new bank?"

"Perhaps, but let's make things difficult for whoever it is."

"Lead the way." Mort said. He followed Ema, her dark green riding habit fading into the darkness that enveloped the street. He pulled both horses along and tethered them inside the property.

The four men look at Ema and Mort with pleading eyes. Their mouths moved, but they heard no sound. She stood at a center point between the statues and drew a sigil in the space. She intoned in an ancient language, "I will take these four."

Immediately a foul smell pervaded the surrounding area, and the sound of something slithering towards them was unmistakable. Then a thin, bony arm came over the side of one statue. What crept over was a lanky old man, almost naked except for a loincloth. He wore a headdress that covered his ears. The blue sandals he wore accentuated his hands and feet that were dyed red. He carried a bowl in one hand. Then a noise like a cat crying echoed around them.

The old man shook his head, and then he lay down on his back, bringing up his knees and resting on one elbow. He placed the bowl on his stomach. With a hand he indicated the empty container. There was no mistaking his movements which asked for something to be placed there.

Ema looked at the figure unflinchingly, "You know these were given to you unwillingly, and you can make no demands."

The old man continued to point to the empty vessel nestled on his stomach.

Ema full lips thinned out in anger, but her voice remained steady. "I will take them now, but I will be generous. I will send a collector to bring you what you desire from those who lied to you and promised what was not theirs to give."

The figure stopped gesticulating and with wide, unblinking eyes nodded once. The cat's crying started again as he slithered once more back over the lion's statue and the stench of rotting blood trailed after him. Then the odor and the sounds faded away.

The four men who'd been straining against unseen tethers, suddenly found they could move and they all congregated around Ema and Mort.

"Help me, help us," they all pleaded in the voices they used when they were among the living.

Ema traced a circle in the air which glimmered fitfully and then enlarged to display an opening. On the other side several figures illuminated in golden light waited. They were transparent, but beckoned with their hands. The men smiled, each seeing someone among the figures they recognized.

Ema said, "Go, and do not look back."

Each one drifted in, their expression joyful and devoid of the fear and anguish they displayed only moments before. The entrance faded until they could not see it.

Mort took Ema's hand and placed it in the crook of his arm and led her away toward where their horses waited nibbling at the sparse grass.

"Ema, I don't know how I understood what you said, but I did. That's the first time. That language has escaped me before."

She smiled at him. "Well, it's only taken you twenty years, that's not bad considering how dead that dead language is."

Mort's smile fled. "What did you negotiate with that thing?"

"I did not negotiate with it, I manipulated it."

"To do what?"

"Flush out the lunatics who are fighting to free the being locked in our cellar, because they think they will control it."

"What do you think will happen next?"

"Mort, they don't need us anymore to babysit this creature. They thought they were ready to harness it, and feed it with the deaths of these men, and what I now realize is the reason for their interest in Hazel."

He looked at Ema and then at the lion statutes, then back at her. "Is it because she transforms into a jaguar?"

"Yes, there is veneration for the jaguar, and there is an aspect of it associated with black sorcery. Sacrificing Hazel would assure its protection over those who for all intents and purposes are acting as the priests did in those ancient cities. Satiated only for a time, it will require more and more. It will never cease to demand tribute, never!"

"Then sending her away is essential, the quicker the better. It will relieve me when we get them on the train tomorrow afternoon."

"Even now they are trying to find out what happened to Gideon Pill. Cutting them off from one of their best foot soldiers, who brought them information about Lane Robinson, has hindered their plans significantly. Now more than ever we must be careful. Desperation in your enemy is a double-edged sword."

17. Paying the Devil His Due

The next day the last preparations for Hazel and Lynne's departure were completed. There was a change in the shop's atmosphere, and Ema knew the source was the artifact she locked away in the bowels of the building. She stayed behind to reinforce the barriers she created against it. Mort accompanied the carriage with both of them to where they would take a ferry to the Oakland Long Wharf then to Alameda where they could board the train.

Mort stayed watching until they were aboard and it was well on its way before returning to the apothecary shop. Once he arrived back, he prepared for the supper at the Occidental Hotel. He dressed in a black tailcoat with knee-length tails, a starched white shirt and bow tie which complimented a double-breasted waistcoat.

Ema dressed in a pink gown, trimmed in maroon flounces. The low neckline exposed her white shoulders, and she wore a red ribbon tied around her neck which trailed behind the gown's bustle flirtatiously.

Gaslights had already been lit when they arrived at the Occidental Hotel. Architects had designed it in the Italianate style. The four story structure towered over other buildings where it sat on the corner of Montgomery and Bush Streets. It was a first-class hotel exuding sumptuous splendor, which welcomed wealthy and famous guests.

Illuminated by a massive chandelier overhead, Ema and Mort sipped champagne as they exchanged introductions with other business owners. Many men came to shake hands with Mort and get a better look at Ema, considered by many a mysterious figure that seldom left the shop. A speculative glint filled their eyes, and they wondered if this was strictly a business partnership as Mort claimed.

Conversations ebbed and flowed around them. Diamonds winked from the throats and ears of women in the crowd. Many of them were the wives and daughters of the Comstock Lode's newly minted silver barons.

Lane Robinson came towards them and introduced himself. He was a middle-aged man, balding with a florid complexion. He asked if they were enjoying themselves and then moved on to ask about their business.

Ema smiled at him. Feathery dark eyelashes offset her green eyes, and he found he could not tear his gaze away. Her thin face, punctuated by full, pink lips titillated his imagination as he wondered what it would feel like to kiss them. The poor man realized she had asked him a question, when she and Mort looked at him expectantly.

"I'm sorry Miss St. George, can you repeat your question?"

"Mr. Robinson, I want to know if you have any partners in this business venture."

"Yes, someone who is a Californian and which has guided me extensively in this endeavor," Lane Robinson looked around and then gestured for someone to join them, "and as luck would have it, here he is now. Marco Robles, the owner of Rancho Las Margaritas. The Robles family has had many interests in California for decades."

The man bowed over Ema's hand and looked up into her face with a half smile on his lips.

Lane Robinson continued, "Marco this is Miss St. George and her partner Mort Peccatum. They own a very well known druggist shop in San Francisco. They have been open for over fifteen years."

133

"I am already acquainted with Don Marco, we met recently as I was traveling in southern California." Mort volunteered.

"This is splendid then. I will leave you to converse about how Metropolitan Bank can assist you in the coming year once the doors open."

Lane Robinson took his leave and moved on to another group of guests.

Marco Robles cleared his throat and shook Mort's hand. "I am glad to find you here Mr. Peccatum as I enjoyed our conversation when you visited my home. I didn't expect you to leave so early the following morning."

"Padre Salazar thought it was prudent and as his escort I saw no reason to contradict his desires."

"Brother Miel, left unexpectedly as well. Were we not hospitable enough?"

"On the contrary, the entire family was very welcoming. Where is your wife so I may introduce her to Miss St. George?"

Marco Robles, paused a moment then chose his words, which despite his effort to appear regretful convinced neither Mort nor Ema. "My poor wife has been feeling ill these last few weeks and could not accompany me. Maria Elena sacrificed herself and agreed to come in her stead. She realizes how important this business enterprise is for our family."

Ema said, "But Mort told me she was expecting a child."

"It turns out no, it was a mistake."

At that moment, a dark-haired woman wearing a black dress, her waist narrow and cinched walked towards them. "Miss St. George may I introduce Maria Elena Robles, she is my father's widow, and you have met Mr. Peccatum already my dear."

"What a pleasure to make your acquaintance, and to see you again Mr. Peccatum." Maria Elena Robles smiled at both of them.

They exchanged pleasantries, but once when Maria Elena touched Ema's arm, she drew back as if it had scalded her. Her eyes shone in amazement tinged with fear when she looked at Ema closer, as if noticing something about the red-haired woman she missed before.

Once when an acquaintance came by to greet Marco and distracted him, the black haired woman openly flirted with Mort alluding to their brief encounter. Ema tried to hide her smile, because she thought it would cause strife between her and Mort, believing like most of the people present that they were lovers.

Ema studied Marco Robles as he conversed with men a few feet away. He was an intelligent and shrewd man, but she also sensed an animal's cunning about his character, and most disturbing a deeply ingrained cruelty in his personality that did not allow any mercy towards others unless there was something to be gained by it. She observed that he loved to talk, and his manners were very smooth, but she wondered how many misjudged his personality as being shallow and just thought of him as a man full of self-importance. She knew already this was a deadly mistake.

The shadows trailing after him confirmed her suspicion they had summoned Notus, the Bring of Familiars for him.

As if sensing Ema's eyes upon him, he stepped back to the group. He leaned towards her and lowered his voice, "I've heard you are quite an accomplished chemist, and that you have clients coming to see you from as far away as New York."

Maria Elena stepped closer and interrupted him, "Marco, trading secrets with Miss St. George?" The woman tossed the ringlets that fell over her shoulder, and Ema could see it irritated her that they excluded her from the conversation.

"On the contrary, she has quite a reputation in being able to produce herbal remedies not found locally. This is quite an asset for an apothecary. I was hoping she would share some of her secrets with me." Marco smiled conspiratorially at Ema.

"I have what's called a green thumb. Right now I am waiting for seeds that are being shipped from South America and British Honduras."

Marco stayed silent a moment, surprised by Ema's statement. She could tell he was trying to assess if there was a hidden meaning in what she said.

Maria Elena responded with a jealous note in her voice, "Then Marco can help you with this. He's visited the area frequently, which is how I met his father. He befriended my stepfather John Dunbar."

Ema could tell that her disclosure irritated Marco. She heightened the friction between them, "Indeed I am familiar with Mr. Dunbar's reputation. He is quite an accomplished mapmaker who accompanied Stephens and Catherwood on their expeditions into the Yucatan Peninsula. I am fascinated by the discoveries they made of so many ruins the jungle swallowed throughout the ages."

Maria Elena bit her lips. She understood her impetuosity caused her to blunder about a subject Marco did not want discussed. Ema then turned her gaze to Mort who was studying Marco's face steadily. When she turned to the man she saw the venomous look, he was shooting at his stepmother.

It was then that Ema felt a tremor of unease quiver through her. She realized the couple stayed next to her and Mort instead of circulating among the other guests. She realized their purpose in attending was strictly to engineer this moment, and there could be only one reason for this.

Suddenly a shout rippled through the crowd. Someone said in a loud voice, "There's been a murder on the ferry!"

"I heard it's Crittenden," another voice called out.

Ema's eyes flew to Mort, and their gaze communicated everything without words. The man named was a well-known and admired lawyer in the city. Only a few days before the governor had appointed him as the Supreme Court Reporter.

"A mad woman on the ferry boat shot A. P. Crittenden." The murmur rippled through the crowd.

The guests swirled around them as everyone tried to find out what occurred.

Ema whispered to Mort, "I have a terrible feeling about this."

"We have to get down to the wharf, and then the train depot." Mort's voice was calm, but his body thrummed with tension. They took the opportunity when Marco and Maria Elena Robles were called away by a group of people talking about the scandal that had just broken.

Mort retrieved his top hat and Ema's short cape from the attendant. He summoned their carriage, and they waited at the front of the hotel. A light mist crept through the streets as their driver brought the carriage forward, leaped down and opened the door. He wore a stovepipe hat and a caped coat. He handed Ema inside and Mort followed.

"Do not worry Sibyllina, I will get you to the wharf right away." The driver said in a quiet voice. "Miguel Angel mentioned that you might need to leave quickly, which is why I stayed close by."

"Thank you Gabriel," she murmured to him.

The sound of the horse's hooves clopping along was the only sound. Mort turned to Ema, "The confusion this caused would have been a perfect cover to take them both."

She nodded, chewing her lower lip. "The timing on this is too suspicious, and if they got on the train, there's no way to find out until they get to the first stop."

Mort said, "There's a small depot the train stops at about thirty minutes after it leaves here. There's a mail packet it picks up, but no passengers. An attendant waits there until the train passes through and then they close shop."

"Is there a telegraph receiver there?" Ema asked.

"Yes, and what's more the agent there owes me a great favor."

Ema spoke up to Gabriel, "Take us to the telegraph office instead."

* * *

Ema waited in the carriage while Mort went to send a telegram. When he returned they started out again to the wharf where the ferry left from.

Mort observed, "I don't think this involves Lane Robinson. I believe he is a silver baron who now wants to become a banker, and that is the extent of his ambitions."

"I agree, however he needed the connection that the Robles family has with many wealthy landowners in the state, which is how they could partner with him on this banking venture. Gideon Pill being his valet was privy to most of his affairs. I am sure he fed them information."

Mort said, "This bank is only a stepping stone for Marco Robles, which is where the relic comes in. He is not willing to bet the success of his plans on luck, desire, and the goodwill of Robinson."

Before they reached the train depot, the throng of people and carriages impeded them from getting closer. The attempted murder of A.P. Crittenden was on everyone lips and the curious wanted to see *El Capitan,* the boat where a heavily veiled woman shot him in the chest.

Mort turned to Ema, "We will wait for word from the depot, or for all we know Hazel turned back and we'll find them waiting for us at the shop."

Ema stayed silent, and then Mort continued, "However I know what you're thinking, a woman who takes the insane measure of shooting a well-known public figure in front of several witnesses, on a boat with no way of escaping is being influenced."

"Mort this is more common than people think. These acts are a distraction from the true target. Who thinks to look twice at two women being forced away when a shooting has just occurred?"

Gabriel came to the window and opened the door. "Sibyllina, let us return to the shop."

She nodded, and then looked at Mort, "We will wait for confirmation from the depot, but I know already what the message will be."

They traveled in silence, and as they pulled up in front of the apothecary shop, a messenger waited on the doorstep.

"Are you Mr. Peccatum?" the young man asked.

"Yes, I am."

"Sir, they have instructed me to give this to you directly."

Mort took the paper from him, and in exchange gave him a coin. Ema joined him, and Miguel Angel opened the door wide. Gabriel clucked to the horse and headed towards the livery stable. The messenger rode off into the murkiness of the swirling fog, and the rattle of retreating hooves echoed through the street.

A lighted lamp waited for them inside, and Mort opened the missive, reading it out loud to Ema, "*Neither of the parties you described was on the train. We made an inspection of the first-class car and extended it throughout the rest of the passengers.*"

18. Don't Look Back

The tall fair-haired man studied his companion, who stared into the flames jumping behind the grate of the fireplace. Gigi nestled on his lap.

"What can we do Ema, wait for them to make the first move?"

"Mort, I think they'll try to negotiate an exchange for the relic, but they only intend to hand over Lynne. They will try to force us to choose between them."

"Then we are clearly at a disadvantage." Mort stated simply.

Her eyes caught and held his. "Perhaps, but not as much as you think."

He leaned forward, and gazed at her, "Ema, tell me what we can do. I can't stand sitting here waiting for them to force our hand and call the shots."

"I am sure they don't know who we are. They suspect us of being high magicians, possibly necromancers but not as adept as they are. They believe we are in over our heads in trying to use the artifact. I doubt they even know what's happened to the four men they sacrificed. They are the incompetent fools that think they'll raise a temple dedicated to this being, disguised as a bank. Their avarice has made them blind, and they think they can control something that has existed for thousands of years."

"Do they think we got rid of Gideon Pill and killed Gallotti?"

"Possibly, but remember Pill made many enemies on the Coast, and so did Gallotti as his enforcer. Dale Stone's death in the fire, could be part of another gang wanting to take over his business, and knew they had to wipe the slate clean."

"God knows there are many that could fall under suspicion for this."

"Also they are not aware that we know what the Order of Primus Sanguis is, and that they brought Bloodletters to work on their behalf."

"Ema wouldn't that Notus demon tell them about you?"

She smiled knowingly and said, "Mort, this thing has allegiance to no one. If they do not complete the ritual to gift the necromancer with a familiar, it will never come again no matter what it's offered. The lack of a familiar will be a disadvantage unsurpassed for anyone working in their circles."

"How do you think Robles got wind of this thing?"

Ema stayed silent for a moment, and then said, "I believe that once Charles Kydd made his discovery, he sent out letters to several parties to see if he could get an expedition financed. I think that is also the reason Alain Beaupre traveled to Belize City. Once he saw what it was, he sent word to us, especially when Kydd asked for an escort into California. Rumors of lost cities full of gold have circulated among archeologists and treasure hunters for years. Any of them could have sent word to John Dunbar and through him it reached the ears of Maria Elena Robles. Without proof, I suspect they proposed Rancho Las Margaritas as a stopping point with the express point of taking it then from Father Salazar."

"Little wonder they looked very surprised when I announced the reason I was there."

Miguel Angel materialized out of the darkness behind them. "Lady Sibyl there is someone downstairs waiting to speak to you. He specified you should come alone."

Ema turned to Mort and said, "Send Omen after this person once they leave." He nodded.

Still dressed in her evening gown, Ema descended the stairs. The swish of her skirts and the ticking clock were the only sounds in the store.

141

A distinguished, middle-aged man stood by the entrance. He was graying at the temples and dressed in a well-tailored suit. He noticed they had not invited him to take a seat.

Ema arched her brow and stared at him questioningly.

"Miss St. George, my name is Peter McDermott." He paused waiting for a response from her but she stayed silent.

"I am an attorney representing Marco Robles. He sent me here with a proposal for you; an offer to complete an exchange. You have an item he desires. He will give you what he has and in addition provide a sum of money so that there are no hard feelings between you and him. I can negotiate this with you however… "

"However?" Ema asked in return.

"I must have an answer tonight. The offer is valid until I leave your shop."

Ema smiled a little, and asked, "So what will happen if you have no response from me? Does that mean he will become uninterested in this trade?"

"I don't know, but Mr. Robles was clear that he will not be as generous as he is at this moment. He also stipulated that if you agree, this exchange can take place tomorrow, and he will bring the money to you in gold."

"Mr. McDermott, do you know about the item he wants from me?"

"No, but he said it is a rare item found in the jungles of British Honduras. He's collected archaeological trophies for many years. I've negotiated sales and trades for him before."

"Does he usually send you at midnight to act as his go-between in these matters?"

The man straightened his jacket, and he answered, "No, however he is eager to return to Rancho Las Margaritas and finish this deal before he leaves. He always recompenses me beyond my usual fee, and I have no cause to complain."

"I will make the exchange only if he agrees to meet at a place of my choosing, I don't like anyone privy to my affairs."

Peter McDermott smiled. "What sum should I say you are asking for?"

Ema stayed silent as if considering his question. She would respond as he expected. "Tell him I want nothing, except the trade, however I hope he will remember this when the Metropolitan Bank opens in the spring and I might need a loan to expand my business."

The man's eyes glinted with a satisfied expression. Greedy merchants were something he was very familiar with. He answered, "A wise decision, Miss St. George. Where is the meeting place?"

"There's a small pier down the coast; an isolated cove close to the lighthouse. We can meet there, an hour before nightfall."

"But why so late in the day?"

"Mr. McDermott, prying eyes can be found where you least expect them. The area is remote, but I do not want any witnesses to our meeting. Also I expect Mr. Robles and his step-mother to both be present, and perhaps one other person of their choosing. I will have my business partner Mr. Peccatum there. I hope you understand my desire for privacy."

The man nodded. "I will relay to Mr. Robles what you want, and I expect he will not object. If there is any point that he is not happy with, I will be in contact with you during the day. No word from me is an indicator that we will meet at the appointed time and place."

Ema added, "Remind Mr. Robles that he has two items that he is bringing to this meeting. If I arrive there and he has not complied with what I described, I will not think twice about leaving and not completing the trade. Is that understood?"

"I would not expect any less."

Out of the murkiness beyond the light of the lamp Miguel Angel came to stand beside him. Startled, the man jumped.

"The time is late sir, and Madame must get her rest." The silver haired man dressed in the brocaded smoking suit ushered him to the front door. Ema stayed silent and watched Peter McDermott look over his shoulder once at her, and then eye Miguel Angel up and down wondering how he approached him without making a sound.

A carriage waited for him, and it departed promptly once he slammed the door shut. From the roof of the three story building a large crow watched with indifferent eyes. It took flight and followed the vehicle as it wound its way through the foggy streets of San Francisco.

19.   Sleep of Kings

In his dream, Mort saw a flock of crows flying over the shop, cawing loudly. In the bedchamber's darkness, something rustled against the curtains that fluttered against the partially open window. A crow cawed once and flew to settle on a small table next to Mort's bed. He opened his eyes and smiled.

"Omen let me see." He whispered. The bird ruffled it ebony feathers and closed its beady eyes.

Mort shut his eyelids and steadied his breathing, emptying his mind. The bird showed him what he wanted to see, the ultimate destination of the man that visited the shop earlier. Its trip there streamed behind his eyes, so quickly he could not make sense of it, but then at the end it slowed and he saw the man being rowed to a small sloop anchored in the bay. The bird perched on a rigging and he saw it from this viewpoint; below Marco Robles spoke to Peter McDermott on the deck. Then the last scene he saw was the ship's name, *My Maria*.

Mort felt Ema stir within him, her voice whispered in his mind, "Sleep now, tomorrow will see us triumph."

* * *

A crack of thunder announced the first drops of heavy rain. In the distance fat, sullen clouds flashed with purplish lights. They rolled and burgeoned towards the city, driving cool winds before it.

When Mort came downstairs, he saw Ema closing the door of a vestibule that led downstairs to the cellar.

"Am I wrong in guessing this weather has to do with your visit in the cellar?"

"Yes, it is not used to negotiating only in being appeased."

Mort's expression became taut, "What does it want from you Ema?"

"First, freedom from the trap the priests tricked it into entering. They emptied the city and left it there alone, unable to influence or cause fear, therefore there were none seeking its favor and willing to meet its demands. It fears this solitude."

"Only that?" Mort asked rhetorically.

Ema smiled and took his hand leading him back upstairs so they could eat breakfast. They ate silently for a few minutes, and then Ema said, "Mort today, I might ask you do things that you might be unhappy about, but you must promise me you will do it without question or hesitation."

Mort put his fork down and looked at Ema, "We work as a team, so why are you being so mysterious?"

"Because we've never come up against something like this before. There are methods which I will use that seem strange to you or… "

"Dangerous." Mort completed the sentence for her.

"Do not be fooled thinking what we've done so often is not dangerous. It always is, even if it's become familiar."

"Ema I have complete trust in you, but I want to protect you at the same time. You may think you will always be the one to safeguard us against danger, but it will be very difficult for me to stand by and allow anyone to harm you."

146

She smiled at him and touched his cheek. "Thank you Mort, but I am impervious to certain things that you are not."

"But you've told me you're human, just like me."

"I am but there are certain things about me that have changed to allow me to exist as I do."

Mort nodded, "You have my promise. But tell me, what is the worst that can happen if this thing falls into the hands of Robles?"

"My belief is that they will sacrifice Hazel within the foundation of the bank. This will grant this being more power than it has now. They will raise the building to look like a bank, but within the structure will be certain aspects, measurements and inscriptions found only in a temple. At the beginning it will be very generous with those who have given it this new home, but it will demand sacrifices, just like it did hundreds of years ago."

Ema continued, "In those times it gave them victory in war, and they sacrificed prisoners, but what happens when there are no lands to conquer or enemies to overcome. The source of sacrificial victims have to come from somewhere, and eventually those chosen are from its own people."

"But these are modern times; they can't just kill someone on the steps of the building." Mort said.

"There are unorthodox ways to satisfy it. As a bank it might drive families into destitution and suicide through duplicity. Those who are in charge can cause a ship to wreck, a mine to collapse and a disease to sweep the city. They hire assassins, thugs or Bloodletters. These calamities were not destined to occur. They will alter the fate of humans who were meant to live longer and instead cause their deaths as an offering."

"You know I will follow your lead and do as you say, no matter if I would do otherwise. You have my word on it."

147

"Thank you, just remember sometimes things are different from what they appear, and there are places that I can go that you cannot follow."

The weather remained strange and unfriendly throughout the morning, and Miguel Angel drove them out in the late afternoon under a steady drizzle. No message came from McDermott so it appeared the plan originally negotiated was in place.

Once they reached the cove, Ema instructed him to keep the carriage out of sight. Mort and her sheltered under the lee of a white-washed boat house next to the pier. She held a satchel made of a black material against her body; the straps would tighten and loosen by turns against her as if it was alive. Sometimes Mort looked at it and he could swear it became a jet black snake. An odor of rotting flesh accompanied the illusion.

The sunlight filtered through sulky clouds, and then they both saw the sloop anchor off in the distance, and a few minutes later a rowboat plunged through the waves towards them.

Ema told Mort to wait for her, and she walked to the end of the pier. There she lay down and dipped her hand into the choppy waves that slapped against the wooden posts. She stood up a few moments later and walked back where he waited for her.

As the rowboat came closer, they made out four persons inside of it. The sailor manning the oars, jumped out and pushed it further onto land.

Mort and Ema walked out to meet the group which comprised Marco and Maria Elena Robles with Lynne between them.

"Ema!" The young girl called out, however Marco Robles shook her arm and interrupted her, "Miss St. George, I am so glad we could agree on this." He pinned his eyes to the satchel strapped across Ema's body. He licked his lips as if expecting a delicious meal.

Mort looked at Maria Elena Robles' eyes that glittered like black jewels in her face. She riveted her gaze on the black bag as well.

"Where is Hazel?" Ema's voice held a silken thread of warning in it.

"She is on the ship. We did not know if you would honor our agreement in full, so we decided just to bring the girl first as assurance you don't just have a piece of rock in there." He pointed at the bag.

"I don't renege on my agreements, but we don't know each other, and I have my doubts about your in."

"That is true we do not know each other." The dark-haired man agreed with her.

"Well since we don't know each other, then we need assurances of good intentions to convince us we will each get what we want. I will go to the boat with the relic, however Mrs. Robles must stay here with Mort until I return with Hazel."

Marco stayed silent, and looked at his companion who shot him a warning glare, leaving no doubt she did not want to remain behind.

Ema's voice was curt and cold. "Mr. Robles, you kidnapped two of my friends, one of them practically a child just to force my hand to trade this item with you. Even now I don't understand why you just didn't send Mr. McDermott with an offer, however here we are now. I do not think I am being unreasonable in my request."

"You are correct, Miss St. George. I wish I could explain my actions, but please don't act innocent, when you know you would have refused me if I had just sent a lawyer with an offer. There are things going on that you have no comprehension of even though you think you do. I am sure you are knowledgeable of some esoteric practices, but you should thank me. I am taking something off your hands beyond your skill. How would I know that you

149

would not become greedy and try to find someone else who would give you more money than what I offered?"

"And what is this special knowledge that you have?" Ema asked softly. "I thought you were just a collector of archeological treasures."

Marco Robles, said with an edge in his voice, "Let us say it is more than your innocuous ability to make plants grow."

Mort then interrupted, "I think I should be the one to go to the ship and fetch Hazel."

"No, I agree with Miss St. George. Just wait here with Doña Robles, and she will return soon and then we can each go our separate ways."

Ema turned to Lynne and said, "Go inside the boat house and wait for us there. Don't come out until one of us comes for you." The girl nodded uncertainly and pulled her arm out of Maria Elena's grasp. They watched the girl walk towards the wooden building and close the door behind her.

Suddenly the straps of the bag against Ema's torso writhed and moved, and the hissing of a snake filled the air.

Marco's eyes shone with excitement, and he moved to take it from Ema, and she stepped back. "No, it stays with me until Hazel is safe."

"Very well."

They walked towards the rowboat, and Ema sensed his surprise at her agility in sloshing through the waves and jumping into the vessel. The sailor rowed hard and plunged them against the waves to the waiting boat. The figures of Mort and Maria Elena became smaller.

Ema broke the silence when her voice sounded over the wind and waves, "Do you ever wonder what became of your overseer Maximo Sandoval?"

Marco Robles tried to hide his surprise at her words, but failed miserably. "They gunned him and some of his men down in a brawl that got out of hand in a nearby town."

"Who told you that?"

"One of them survived the gunfight and returned with the story. Strangely enough a bull gored him to death a few days later. Sometimes there is no escaping your fate. But why would you ask me this Miss St. George?"

"Because that story is a lie. Maximo Sandoval tried to steal the relic from Mort and Father Salazar in San Diego, and a hellish creature intervened and killed your overseer. Maria Elena Robles instructed Maximo to retrieve this," she patted the satchel, "and bring it back to her."

Marco just stared at her. He knew that she spoke to the truth. Those methods sounded like something that Maria Elena would concoct. She might appear to be subservient to him, but he knew she wanted to be in control of everything. But time enough later to deal with his step-mother; he envisioned throwing her overboard and replacing her with the red-headed woman in his bed.

"I have underestimated you Miss St. George. I see that you are more knowledgeable about what you carry than I originally thought."

"If anything I am more cautious than either of you." Ema replied mysteriously.

They came alongside the sloop and a sailor on boat helped her to board. Once they were all on deck, Ema turned to him and said, "Bring Hazel and let's get this done. Once we're on shore, they can carry Mrs. Robles back to the ship."

Hazel heard Ema's voice, and she hurried out of the cabin and came to her side. She hugged her and said, "I am so glad to see you.

The ocean is not my friend, and I cannot wait until my feet are on solid ground."

Ema gazed at her, and said, "Trust me you will be safe no matter what."

Hazel nodded, understanding there was a hidden meaning in her words, but she could not still her heart which thudded with fear.

Marco Robles smiled with self satisfaction. "Miss St. George, your piece of information of what my father's wife did to outmaneuver me, confirmed that I am better off without her. Both of you though are invaluable. Come away with me and I will shower you with riches beyond your wildest imaginings."

Ema remained quiet as if considering his proposal. She walked away and looked out over the sea. Hazel stayed closed to her.

She turned back to Robles and said, "My answer is no. Hazel and the four men on board are to row to shore. I will stay here with you until they come back. Then and only then, will I turn over this bag to your possession."

The man chuckled in cynical amusement. "And what will you do, if my answer is no, that both of you will stay here with me and I will order the men to sail away? Will you both swim to shore?"

Ema took the straps from around her shoulder and held it over the side of the boat, the gray-green waves appearing to reach out for it. Marco's smile disappeared, and he snarled, "What are you doing?"

"Order your men into the boat and tell them to row Hazel to shore. If they return, it will be their choice."

Ema turned to the four sailors standing behind Marco. They looked uncertainly at him and then at Ema. Being sailors the worsening weather had not escaped their attention. The vessel rocked hard as the waves increased.

"Think well Marco, otherwise I will drop this into the sea, and good luck on finding it afterward. Stormy weather and currents will drag it to who knows where."

Then a fetid odor of a decomposing body settled like a cloud among them unaffected by the gusts of wind. Snuffling, pig-like grunts came from the bag. All the men stepped to the far side of the ship; some of them crossed themselves.

"Wait!" Robles shouted to her. "Think a moment Miss St. George, if you don't want to stay with me, I will deliver you and Hazel to San Francisco. We will sail there, and Mr. Peccatum no doubt will take Maria Elena and the girl to the city. I would like you to accompany me, but the artifact is more important. I have no interest in forcing either of you to stay with me. Do not be hasty!"

"This is not open to negotiation; if you keep talking, we'll jump into the sea with this thing and take our chances on swimming to shore."

"You are mad!" The man shouted at her.

Then whatever was in the satchel bulged the sides out and snarled. The sailors turned wide eyes to Marco. One of them, an older man who was the captain, said, "Don Robles we are leaving, there is something unholy in that bag. Look at the seas, the way the weather has become dangerous." Two of the men stepped down into the rowboat which bobbed high on the waves. A third one took Hazel and ushered her to the rowboat. Ema could see they were desperate to leave.

"Go Hazel." She said simply.

"Be damned all of you!" Marco shouted; a trickle of sweat started down his cheek despite the cool weather.

The remaining men swarmed onto the boat. It charged towards shore as two of them manned the oars; hunched over in their exertion to put as much distance between themselves and the sloop as possible.

Ema kept the bag hanging over the turgid waters until she saw the distant figure of Hazel jump off and make her way towards shore.

She turned to Marco, "Remember, I offered you various times to stop this."

The man's eyes were full of murderous intent and rage at being thwarted. "What do I care what you've offered me you bitch, just give me that bag, now!"

She tossed it to him, and he caught it in midair and then instantly dropped it as a howl of pain erupted from his mouth. He looked at his scalded hands which were turning red; watery bubbles rose on the skin of his palms.

"Isn't it everything you expected?" Ema asked. "It wants its freedom. It expects you to blister your hands in the process and you should be glad of it in order to prove your adoration."

He stared down at the package at his feet which throbbed and pulsed as if there was something alive inside of it. The pain shooting along his nerve endings stopped him from retrieving it.

The sails on the ship snapped and fluttered. Ema's voice rose so he could hear her over the whistling of the wind. "What are you thinking? Are you wondering why it's not content with all the sacrifices you committed in its name just to welcome it?"

Marco Robles stayed silent, the first inkling of doubt creeping into his cult-like belief that the trapped being would reward him.

Ema laughed mirthlessly, "You didn't think the pain of those you killed would be enough, right? I know you murdered them with your own hands, because it demanded this from you."

He squatted down, and with a finger touched the material, and he drew it back quickly, the smell of burning flesh filling the air. He stood up slowly, trying to keep his feet under him as the boat lurched against the waves.

"The only way off this boat is with my help, because those sailors will not be returning."

He eyed Ema now discerning something that he missed before. He realized that he saw what he expected to see; a beautiful woman, owner of a small, profitable shop who dabbled in occult matters, but was no threat to him. However, only a few moments ago she held the artifact strapped against her body with no discomfort.

Her next words sent a disquieting premonition thrumming through his body. "Your time is scant, Notus the Bringer of Familiars once gone will never return. I believe you are realizing your devotion to this creature entails quite a lot of pain. Do you think those priests who left it to be forgotten in the ruins of their magnificent cities did it for no reason at all?"

"Who are you?" He asked.

"It is of no consequence now, but you must decide, your life or the reliquary."

"Why?" he shouted at her over the wind.

"Because I'm sinking the boat, is that plain enough for you?"

Then his eyes widened when he saw hands and then a pale, shimmering arm grasped the edge of the deck. "Sibyllina." A whispery voice called out. Then on the other side, other hands with glistening, reflective scales appeared.

Ema came to where the voice called out; she kneeled down and saw large, silver eyes looking up at her. Sharp teeth lined her mouth, below a barely formed nose, but she smiled with delight. Her delft colored skin shone with the seawater and her greenish hair floated behind her. Beyond it the flap of her wide tail agitated the water.

"Cymatilis thank you for answering my call."

"Sister, Melusine sent me in her stead. What is on this ship that causes this disturbance to the seas?"

"An evil thing, antithetical to life, but I have no choice but to trap it here."

Ema heard steps behind her, curiosity driving Marco to come and see who she conversed with. When he saw the mermaid's face, he stumbled backwards.

Ema turned back and said, "Take this man to the shore. I would give him to you under other circumstances, but I have promised him to another. I can only warn you he will not come willingly."

Cymatilis threw back her head and laughed which sounded like a bell's peal. "We will make his fear turn into desire."

Ema nodded. She stood up and stripped off her dress until she stood clothed only in a thin, muslin chemise. Marco Robles just stared at her. Then she beckoned to him, and he stood up and came to her. The man in him felt a desire for the barely dressed woman who stood on the tilting deck as if she had been born to it, while there was another part of him which stirred and recoiled from her. It was a part of him that urged him to take part in the darkest rituals, never expressing regret or mercy for those he slaughtered on altars that were always damp with sticky blood.

Ema's red hair became undone and whipped behind her like a flag. "Look down," and she pointed to the waves.

Below he saw two beautiful women, one with golden locks and the other one's hair was black as jet. Strange, exotic flowers hung around their necks, and below he saw the full swell of their breasts just below the waterline. They smiled and then laughed their eyes full of promise; without another word he jumped into the sea.

One grabbed him by the scruff of his coat, and the other held his arm. With a swish of their tails they swam off towards shore, pulling him along barely keeping his face above the water.

Ema then turned and pushed her hand, palm first into thin air where it disappeared and she pulled out her sword Zeruko Neskamea.

THE PATH TO PURGATORY

A black, viscous stain spread out from under the satchel, and whatever was inside bulged even larger, and the stench of death was so strong that the surrounding tempest could not diminish it.

Ema held the pommel of the sword with both hands. It sparkled with cerulean flames and vibrated producing a low hum. She intoned in a deep, echoing voice "Rima," and then pointed the sword down into the deck. A crack appeared; thin at first and with the sound of snapping wood it widened.

The creature snarled as if understanding what her intentions were, but bound inside its trap all it could do was voice its protest.

"Rima!" she repeated in a stronger voice that thundered over the sound of the gusts of wind that tossed the ship. Clouds rolled in from the horizon over the sea, flashing and winking with greenish light.

Seawater bubbled up and other areas in the ship protested against the intruding ocean. The waves frothed over the deck, and the noises coming from the relic intensified. Not only did the screams of animals emanate from it but also human voices moaning in anguish.

Ema felt the boat shudder under her feet as seawater filled up the hold and the cabin. Then a grinding sound rumbled from the mast and rigging, and they tilted towards the ocean. Then Ema felt nothing underneath her feet, and she thrust her sword into the other dimensional pocket where she kept it. She felt a sucking motion underneath her as the ship surrendered to the sea, and she swam in place surrounded by debris from the ship that floated around her.

Cymatilis appeared next to her. "The man has reached shore and your avatar is standing guard over him and a dark-haired woman."

Darkening clouds lowered down over the water and the waves tossed even harder. The mermaid smiled at Ema, "Sibyllina, despite my wish it were otherwise you are a creature of the earth and your lips are turning blue."

Suddenly a tentacle broke the surface and shot up into the air. The mermaid screamed in alarm. At the same moment Ema felt something wrap around her ankle and jerk her downwards into the throbbing water. She looked up and saw the waves rolling above her. Her descent halted as Cymatilis swam down to her and grabbed her around the waist, trying to pull her out of the grasp of the appendage. Ema looked down and her vision changed to accommodate being underwater. She saw that a black mass writhed around the wreckage of the ship which had fallen on a ledge. Below it murky depths stretched beyond what she could see.

The mermaid then attacked the tentacle biting into it with her sharp teeth, the dark-haired mermaid that accompanied her joined in. However it would not release Ema's leg.

Ema knew that somehow the seawater had degraded the trap that held it, and it was seeking to claim vengeance against her. It mimicked one form of life found in the ocean, corrupted in form though.

She could hold her breath longer than most humans, but she could not breathe underwater. The thing jerked her down again. The mermaids continued to bite it viciously. Ema looked up, and she only saw her red hair streaming above her, and the surface where lay salvation was receding. She tried swimming up, but it held her fast and she could not break away. In response to her movement it tightened its hold around her calf.

She looked down and saw the mermaids stare into the lightless depths where a gigantic shadow loomed. They let go of the tentacle and swam away, and Ema wondered what it was they feared so much they would abandon her.

Ema felt the lack of oxygen and coldness of the water invade her being, and dizziness made her lose her sense of direction. She tried to focus her vision to see what drove away her companions, but all she saw was a bulky shadow shoot towards her. Then she felt powerful arms catch her around the waist, and her hands settled on massive shoulders that rippled with muscles. A mouth covered hers and filled her lungs with air. The figure released her, and she felt a mighty movement below her and the tentacle's grip loosened.

Cymatilis appeared and pulled her around the waist, and with a mighty swish of her tail took her to the surface. Ema coughed and took gulps of air.

"Who was that?" she gasped out.

"His name is Immane, and he is an ancient merman. I have never seen him, only heard tales about him. Sibyllina you must be very special if he came to your side."

Then a mighty head broke the surface, and Ema was looking into the face of a man with eyes like silver dollars, small slits for his nose and a large, expressive mouth full of sharp teeth that enabled him to eat many types of marine life. His blue grayish skin shimmered with the sheen of water and the soft scales that covered his body winked with pearly hues. His hair hung to wide shoulders rippling with muscles.

"Thank you." Ema murmured to him. "I am in your debt, for without your intervention I would have perished." She looked at him in wonderment because for all the hundreds of years she existed she had been in ignorance of his existence. "How is it I have never heard your name?"

"Lady Sibyl I am well acquainted with yours."

"Will you not tell me more about yourself?"

He shook his head, "Now is not the time, you must leave the water and bring up the temperature of your body or you will die. I have sent the ship off the ledge, and the abomination that held you fell with it into a deep trench."

159

Ema felt a tremor course through her body, and dizziness swept over her. The dark-haired mermaid held her and swam towards the shore.

Cymatilis glanced at Immane and cast him a flirtatious look. She never felt so enraptured with a creature like herself. For once she felt the effect that she caused human men to feel.

"Immane why did you come to help Sibyllina? How did you know of her plight?"

Perhaps this will help you comprehend. He transformed to his pleasing human form that all Mer people were capable of. His shoulder length hair turned a brilliant red, and his eyes took on a gray green color that glimmered with specks of blue. Cymatilis saw Ema's face in a masculine cast, and she said, "Now I understand."

"She is one of mine." he said before taking Cymatilis by the hand, and they both dived under the now quieting waves.

20.   The Promised Ones

The mermaid brought Ema into shallow water. She turned to her and said through trembling lips, "What is your name? There is something familiar about you, but I've never seen you before."

"My name is Quinox, my mother is Melusine. She has told me the story of how you saved us both when the Greek sailors caught her in their nets when she was ready to give birth to me."

"Thank you Quinox." Ema said with a voice full of gratitude. "Be on your way then."

The mermaid smiled at her, turned and with a splash of her iridescent tail disappeared into the crashing waves.

Ema stumbled out of the surf. The clouds parted to allow a few rays of remaining daylight to illuminate the beach. The mermaid had brought her to the far side of where the boat house stood. She came around the corner of the building and found Mort, with a revolver in his hand standing watch over Marco and Maria Elena Robles who sat on the sand. Hazel and Lynne huddled together under the overhang of the boathouse's roof.

"Ema!" they all called out when they saw her.

Mort came to her side, took off his coat and draped it around her shoulders.

In a shaky voice she asked Mort, "Where are the sailors from the ship?"

"They high-tailed it out of here, almost running down the road, but the captain asked that we not mention what happened because they planned to leave San Francisco quickly and head back to San Diego. I think this is not the first time they've witnessed victims being kidnapped and held on the ship. They do not want to swing on a rope because they're brought up on charges of being accomplices."

"So what are you going to do, shoot us?" Marco Robles interrupted them, calling out from where he sat. Maria Elena Robles looked at them with piercing eyes full of hatred.

Ema's tone was contemptuous, "No, you are free."

Maria Elena commented ragefully, "They'll shoot us in the back."

The soft clop of a horse's hooves sounded out, and the carriage steered by Miguel Angel appeared over a slight rise where a narrow road led to where they waited.

Marco looked at his companion with distaste.

The carriage halted and Miguel Angel opened the door beckoning to Hazel and Lynne who went to him with hurried steps. Little Gigi jumped out, her hackles standing on end as she stared out into the shadows.

Then far off in the dunes an inhuman cry rang out. It started out as a deep growl and ended in a shrill scream. Marco and Maria Elena both stood up, worry now etched on their faces. They eyed the carriage which they knew did not have any space to carry them.

"What is that?" Maria Elena asked, the mockery in her voice had disappeared.

"Ask Marco, he sent it to my home to kill Father Salazar." Ema said in a dispassionate tone.

"What is she talking about?" the black-haired woman turned to her companion.

Marco's face was defiant when he said, "At least send a hired carriage out here to pick us up."

Miguel Angel turned the carriage around, and Mort jumped to a pedestal on the back of it. Lynne already sat on Hazel's lap to make space for Ema.

Ema looked off into the windswept dunes that were quickly fading into the gloominess of twilight

"I would if I could find any that would come out here in the night, but even if I found anyone, they would not find you."

"Why not? I will not tramp back into the city like some sailor or miner that doesn't even have a horse to ride on."

The shrill cry echoed again off in the distance.

Marco smiled sardonically, "Do you think I'm scared of what made that sound? Remember what you just said, I was the one that sent it."

It was Ema's turn to smile, "And you believe it's still under your control? I've freed it, and it's hungry."

If he had not witnessed what he saw on his boat earlier, he would not believe what she said, but now there was no doubt he underestimated her. In fact, he did not know what to make of her. He recognized a hard truth for someone with his ego, which was that he was only an apprentice standing before a powerful master.

Then the disquieting call of crying cats sounded close by. Mort's eyes met Ema, because they both knew what approached them. She said to him, "They are about to learn a hard lesson that they will never profit from."

Then the stench of rotting corpses came among them as if it was a solid thing.

"Freed what? What is she talking about?" Maria Elena Robles asked Marco, hysteria rising in her voice.

"How much do you want Miss St. George?" Marco said in a voice rough with anxiety.

"I want nothing." She replied.

"Mr. Peccatum, what of you? I will give you any sum you mention. You have been to one of my ranches, there are two others, so you know I have the funds to back my offer."

"Robles, I want nothing." Mort answered shortly.

163

"You cannot leave us here." Maria Elena said in a shaky voice.

"Yes, I can. Just stay on the road and it will take you back into the city. Perhaps you can conjure a protector, but I doubt any will answer your summons." Ema said.

"But you know that we don't stand a chance." Marco advanced towards them.

Mort pulled out his colt revolver and aimed it at him. "Ema get inside the carriage."

Then he turned to Robles, "I'll shoot you in the gut, and let you linger out here if you take another step."

"Mort, please, do not leave me." Maria Elena pleaded with him. He looked at her with indifferent eyes.

"Yes, I am." he replied.

Ema climbed into the carriage and closed the door. Mort jumped on the back, and Miguel Angel clucked to the horse and it pulled away. A dense fog was coming in from the ocean, and soon it would be difficult to see more than a few feet in front of them. Lynne protested they were leaving Gigi behind. Hazel said in a soft voice that the little dog would be safe.

When they cleared the rise, and the road sloped downward, they heard the cry of the creature coming closer. The howl of a wolf followed it.

Mort kept looking around him into the landscape wrapped in darkness. Close by he saw the flash of white fur as a large wolf-like creature loped along, guarding their progress as they sped down the road towards the city.

Miguel Angel's calm voice drifted back to where he was, "Mort, do not fear, we will be safe, just take care of Lady Sibyl when we arrive at the shop."

* * *

They all slept in and gathered in the small dining room of Ema's apartment for a late breakfast. Gigi gorged as each person at the table fed her a tidbit. Soledad came and brought the newspaper to Mort. She pointed at a headline below one concerning the murder of A.P. Crittenden by Laura Fair. He read it to those at the table:

> *"Mysterious Disappearance Accompanies Strange Weather*
>
> *An unexpected storm took an unusual course moving southward along the California coast line, a course it has never taken before.*
>
> *Marco Robles and his father's widow Maria Elena Robles set sail on their sloop My Maria earlier in the day when the weather was still fair. They, along with four crew members are missing, and they fear their boat foundered. Marco Robles is an investor in Lane Robinson's Metropolitan Bank and the Robles family have three sizeable ranches in the southern end of the state.*
>
> *Heavy rain covers the state from the northern boundary line to San Luis Obispo, and it has been heavy in the Sacramento valley and extending into the interior. It has been accompanied by a decided cold wave in the Rocky Mountains, extending into Utah and Nevada. There is a freezing temperature as far as Carson City where it was snowing yesterday.*
>
> *This unsettled weather is being blamed for the disappearance of Robles' vessel, and storm signals are on display from here to Eureka."*

Rain thrummed against the window, and fog pressed like a gray sheet against the glass. The fire crackled in the silence, and they all thought of what transpired the day before on the beach. The conversation resumed of inconsequential things, and Hazel asked Lynne to accompany her downstairs to the workroom to help organize some plants brought in from the roof. She understood that Mort and Ema wanted to converse alone.

"Do you think they survived?" Mort asked Ema.

"No, they were the promised ones. I doubt there is even a scrap of clothing to be found."

"Ema what about that thing that killed Charles Kydd, aren't others in danger from it?"

Her voice held a quiet emphasis when she answered, "Mort, this creature is not a demon, and they brought in it from another dimension. It rarely hunts humans. It will head into the mountains seeking cooler weather and the animals that inhabit the area. I am sure throughout the years there will be stories of strange sightings but there is plenty of uninhabited land where it can exist and hurt no one."

"What about Lynne?"

"We will proceed with our plan to take her to St. Louis, but I will go in Hazel's stead to explain everything to her family. Based on what she told me, it will not surprise them to learn that Gideon Pill had a hand in the murder of his wife. I believe they would remain quiet to protect Lynne, especially when I assure them that Mildred's killer has met his own end."

"What about Robles' conspirators, I doubt he worked alone?"

"No he did not, but what is that saying about cutting off the head of the snake; we will take advantage of their disorganization and make sure they don't regroup."

Mort stayed silent and then asked, "What about the relic?"

"It's now in a deep trench, and the worst that can happen is unusual weather in that area or that vessels will inexplicably disappear. Its power is curtailed as long as it's trapped there, and I hope that is where it stays."

"If it was recovered and brought to the surface, what would happen?"

Ema paused and said in a subdued voice, "Death and destruction on a large scale."

"It sounds like someone came to help." Mort said.

"Yes the Mer people, they are invaluable allies."

The conversation drifted to other topics. They sat at the table making plans for her trip and the need to reopen the house and repair the damage to the storeroom. It was a while later that Soledad appeared with a folded message.

Mort opened it and said, "It's from Paul Kane."

"What does it say?"

He read, "*Two dead bodies found horribly mutilated near the lime quarry on Mount Diablo. Three large stones and a large stick covered in blood lay near the man. Someone smashed in his head and they drew a rope around his neck three times. Nearby was the body of a woman whose neck bore marks of having been bruised by some blunt instrument, perhaps a man's clenched hand and the left arm was much lacerated. A magnificent gold watch was still resting in a belt about her waist bearing the initials upon the inner case, "J.C.R." Her garments were of fine texture though badly torn and her general appearance denoted her as having been a lady of wealth. They have hit no clue upon either to their identity or the perpetrators of the deed. Both had the insignia of P.S. in secreted parts of their bodies. They are held here at the undertaker in hopes someone will identify them. As you can understand I am alarmed after my last experience. Your servant, PK.*"

"So it begins." Ema murmured.

Mort raised questioning eyes to her.

"There is a powerful person who wishes to remove all clues that will lead to them, especially the ones that can talk. We are not done yet with this matter and in the coming months or years it will resurface."

"Undoubtedly."

167

"Please go see Paul and warn him those cadavers should not have contact with any blood, fresh or otherwise. Even a bleeding cut will reanimate them."

Mort stretched out his tall form and reached for his hat. He smiled at her and then walked downstairs. Ema heard the bell on the front door jingle when he left. She sat there for a moment lost in thought. She knew that dead men tell no tales, but none would be safe if the sea gave up its secrets.

21.   April 18, 1906

TYBEE ISLAND, GEORGIA

A drive shadowed by oak trees led to a cottage overlooking the Atlantic Ocean. Ema and Mort sat on the raised porch that extended across the house. They finished breakfast, and the red-haired woman eyed her pocket which dozed in his chair, something he did more frequently now that he was about to celebrate his 71st birthday. This was one reason she sold her apothecary shop in Savannah and moved permanently to this small home they used to vacation at during the summer months. She looked at the man sitting next to her, and she could not deny the fact that his once blonde, lion's mane was mostly gray. One of his knees had grown stiff and gave him pain in the morning. He also complained of a dull throbbing along the scar where a bullet had deeply grazed the side of his skull many years ago.

Ema took the newspaper and unfolded it. Blazoned across the front page was the headline:

AN EARTHQUAKE WRECKS HEART OF SAN FRANCISCO
Worse Shock Ever Felt on the Pacific Coast
Many Victims Reported
Lack of Water Crippled Fight with Flames
Terror and Excitement
Hundreds Killed and Probably 1,000 Injured
Entire Waterfront Now Burning.

She looked at a large black-and-white picture of Market Street in flames. Her eyes filled with tears and she knew in her heart the reliquary no longer resided among the bones of the ship *My Maria*.

www.ingramcontent.com/pod-product-compliance
Lightning Source LLC
Chambersburg PA
CBHW020910180626
46816CB00007BA/2334